Dear Reader,

First, I want to thank you for taking *Night Pleasures* off the bookshelf! Just like you, I love to be entertained by a strong, sexy man who spices my fantasies, something that's naturally led me to want to try my hand at Sensual's sexiest books, the SIZZLING miniseries.

In this story, code-cracker Edison Lone solves word puzzles, and he loves discovering and fulfilling a woman's secret passions. When he's asked to crack the code of a steamy, erotic diary, how can he and his fantasising lady-love share anything *but* pleasure at night?

Needless to say, I truly hope you'll laugh, cry and be breathless with suspense—all in anticipation of that final wonderful moment when you just know these two people are perfect for each other!

Enjoy!

Jule McBride

Look out for the next Sensual Romance™ novel by Jule McBride, *Naughty by Nature*, also in the SIZZLING mini-series, on sale in September.

NIGHT PLEASURES

by

Jule McBride

MILLS & BOON®

First published in Great Britain 2002
by Harlequin Mills & Boon Limited,
Eton House, 18-24 Paradise Road, Richmond, Surrey TW9 1SR

ISBN 0 263 83283 X

21-0802

Printed and bound in Spain
by Litografia Rosés S.A., Barcelona

Prologue

"WE'VE REACHED A CRISIS point," she said, pretending to nibble a sandwich, her lips barely moving. "We've got to get rid of Edison Lone. Now."

He sat beside her on a park bench, wearing one of his many finely tailored suits, the uniform of what he was—a major power broker in the most power-hungry city in America. As her low, husky voice rippled through him, he decided that some men would be threatened by her raw sensuality, others by her intelligence, and still others by the power the woman wielded in Washington; he was simply aroused. He was her lover, and each word affected him like a slow-drip aphrodisiac feeding straight into his veins. Slowly, he turned a page of the classified ads in this morning's free tabloid. "Any suggestions about how to rid ourselves of Lone?"

"Oh," she purred. "I've got a few."

"Care to share them?"

"Only if you're good."

A mental vision of how she'd looked last night, stepping naked from the octagonal swimming pool in her estate in Arlington, made it difficult to hide his surging arousal. "Last night I *was* good, wasn't I?"

"Or bad, depending on which way you look at it."

"I looked at it from every angle."

"You mean you looked at *me* from every angle?" she murmured.

"That, too. And I didn't see any part of you complaining."

Her trace of a smile vanished. "No, but we'll both be complaining if Edison Lone gets any closer to finding out what we're up to."

Actually, they'd be tried for treason. Glancing from the tabloid, he stared past a fountain toward Pennsylvania Avenue. "Speaking of breaches in security, are you sure you weren't followed?" While they interacted in business contexts, they'd never been seen together socially.

"Of course I wasn't. But we had to meet. Phone lines are never secure. And we've got to get Edison Lone out of the picture."

"Permanently?"

She considered. "No...at least not yet. That would look suspicious."

"Later?"

"Later, if we have to, we'll make...arrangements."

"*Permanent* arrangements?" he echoed, his neck prickling with a sudden chill. "You think the man's that dangerous to us?"

"He could figure out what we're doing. He's the best code cracker in Washington."

Edison Lone had also been a child prodigy, an early Harvard graduate, and was a Mensa member. He was more patriotic than George Washington, too. "Rumor has it he'd send his own children to the electric chair if he thought they were messing over Uncle Sam."

"Not his children. He doesn't have any. Nor ex-wives. He's a confirmed bachelor," she told him.

"Maybe we've found his Achilles' heel. With any luck he's secretly gay. We could use that against him, couldn't we?"

"Edison Lone? Gay?" She nearly choked. "The man possesses so much testosterone he's probably taking supplements."

"I said *secretly.*"

"Everybody knows he likes women."

The words rankled. "*You* know that?"

"I'm just offering common knowledge about the man."

He sighed heavily, well acquainted with Edison Lone's considerably thick dossier. Six foot one, thirty-five years old and blessed with jet-black hair and blue eyes, Lone had once upon a time been a foster child who'd exhibited such unusual aptitude in school that he'd wound up getting a first-rate education privately subsidized by benefactors. Off the record, Edison Lone was reputed to be one of those enviably rare, lucky men who drew women to him like an MRI magnet.

The man sighed again. He'd really hoped Edison Lone might be gay. But even *he'd* heard the female gossip around Washington about Lone being a wizard under the bedsheets.

Her husky voice broke into his reverie. "He's convinced someone's using the classified ads to make contacts and sell information from IBI, so he could find out it's us. This morning, he said he might take his suspicions to CIIC."

"If CIIC investigates, we're toast. Did you try to talk him out of it?"

She nodded affirmatively.

They'd probably talked alone, he thought, in one of those high-tech conference rooms laid out with imported coffee and a fancy silver service. In addition to the stab of jealousy and the threat of being exposed as a traitor by Edison Lone, he decided the mind-boggling acronyms in Washington were enough to make a man's head hurt. IBI were the initials for the Internal Bureau of Information, the organization that employed Edison Lone. CIIC, the Center for International Informational Control, was the watchdog organization that kept its eye on IBI.

"We'd better do something soon," she said. "Otherwise he'll realize we're selling information from IBI's database."

The database included strategic plans for every national emergency from biomedical disaster to nuclear attack, and once more buyers were in place, they could finish unloading what they had to sell. "We've got to get Lone out of the picture," she repeated. "And without drawing attention to everything he's been working on for the past year."

"All we need is a week, then we can leave the country."

"Only a week," she agreed.

He thought of their new identities, passports and disguises, then of the walled compound they'd purchased in Bali, with its private, white-sand beaches and crystal-clear cerulean waters. "We've worked too hard to let anyone get in our way now."

"Can we get Edison Lone assigned to a case that would occupy his time? Just for a week?" she asked.

"If you're sure he's not gay, I've got a solution."

She frowned as if conflicted. "The distraction's female?"

He nodded. "Her name's Selena Silverwood."

"Never heard of her."

"Of course you haven't. She's a secretary at IBI."

"They're *assistants*," she reminded him, ever the diplomat.

He shrugged. "Whatever. The point is, she's been bringing a highly personal erotic diary to work—"

"An erotic diary? To work?" She stared at him. "Why?"

"A New York house is publishing her erotic fantasies as a book titled *Night Pleasures*. Originally, it was a personal diary full of her private fantasies."

"Fantasies?"

He nodded. "Involving a French courtesan's sexual encounters with a mysterious marquis. The book's being released next June, and the publishers have asked her to do some of her own editing. Anyway, because she was working on something other than IBI documents on IBI time, the diary came to the attention of our office. Naturally, we had to check her out."

"Naturally." She smiled. "Just in case she really was stealing information from IBI. And you found?"

"That *Penthouse Letters* has nothing on this girl."

"Her fantasies are that hot?"

"Satan himself would beg for ice cubes."

"So, you think this woman can turn Edison Lone's head and keep him occupied for a week?"

He hedged. "Selena Silverwood's not much to look at."

She sighed in exasperation. "Edison Lone goes for pretty."

"True. But there's something he likes more than pretty."

"Ah," she guessed. "Codes that other cryptanalysts have failed to crack. Still, I'm not following you."

He flashed a smile. "We'll make a copy of Selena Silverwood's erotic diary and tell him it's in secret code. We'll pretend CIIC thinks she's using those steamy stories to smuggle sensitive information out of IBI."

She shook her head. "Too far-fetched. C'mon, do you really think we can pass off a woman's erotic fantasies as something she's written in secret code?"

"Stranger things have happened in Washington."

"True," she admitted. "And if it worked, Selena Silverwood could fall under suspicion for stealing from IBI."

"However briefly," he replied. "But that's perfect. We only need to occupy Edison Lone for a week. Just long enough that he can't keep analyzing those classified ads—and start suspecting us."

She looked unconvinced. "I don't know. He's too smart to fall for this, isn't he?"

"Not if he's sure the woman's a traitor."

Another slow smile curled her lips. "You're right. His Achilles' heel is definitely his patriotism. If he thinks CIIC's involved, he might believe us. Besides, we don't have much choice but to try this." She sighed, switching the subject. "Do you know why I love you?"

"Because I'm brilliant and deviant?"

She nodded. "Yes. And because Edison Lone, as much as I've sometimes enjoyed his company, is becoming a thorn in my side. I knew you could get rid of him."

"Lover," he murmured, "a rose such as yourself should never have a thorn."

1

THAT'S WHAT I LOVE about words, Edison Lone thought ruefully. Unlike women, they came with handbooks of rules and regulations. Dictionaries and grammar books told you how to deal with them. They were dependable. Reliable. Predictable. And because he hated to see words spliced and diced, as he so often did while cracking codes for the government, he was extremely careful when choosing his own. He uttered a long, succinct string of expletives.

His boss, Eleanor Luders, looked vaguely alarmed. "Excuse me?"

"C'mon," he chided, appalled that anyone would require him to research a low-level assistant such as Selena Silverwood right now. "You don't really need a professional code cracker for this job, do you?" His deliberate blue-eyed gaze panned the conference table, landing on Eleanor, a tall woman with white-blond, shoulder-length hair, wearing a practical gray suit; then on *her* boss, Newton Finch, a fifty-year-old ex-New Yorker who was wearing rumpled gray pinstripes; then finally on *his* boss, Carson Cumberland, who looked like a replica James Bond, the Pierce Brosnan version, also gray-clad. Combined, they seemed about as cheery as the rainy April sky over D.C., and judging from the grim smiles, silver didn't line the clouds, either.

"Care to sit?" Eleanor asked, ignoring his question.

"Love to." Instead of dropping his tall, broad-shouldered body into one of the plush chairs around the conference table, Edison continued, "Like I said, I found some suspicious personal ads in one of the free tabloids. The ads are for sexual bondage, but references to getting tied up—with whom, where and when—have convinced me that somebody's using the ads to negotiate the sale of confidential information, maybe from IBI."

Newton looked concerned. "Have any proof?"

"If I did, I'd have taken further action."

Eleanor's glance reminded him not to antagonize superiors. *Glance of censure duly noted,* thought Edison. *Duly ignored.* "I do have a hunch, though," he added, deciding there was nothing he hated more than wasting American tax dollars haggling with the brass. "So, right now, investigating an assistant would be an inefficient use of my time. Look..." Softening his voice, he tried to sound diplomatic. "Forget Selena Silverwood. My time's better spent analyzing the classifieds."

The suddenly flirtatious spark in Eleanor's liquid blue eyes made Edison regret sleeping with her seven years ago. Chalk it up to a Christmas office party when he'd been young, green and still getting his feet wet at IBI. He'd been wearing the proverbial lampshade on his head, and Eleanor, who'd been an administrator in another division, had looked like a million bucks. Edison never imagined he'd wind up transferred to her division years later, and now he counted himself lucky that she'd recently gotten married.

"You've always proved yourself unusually intuitive," she purred, her marriage doing nothing to curb the seductive tone she used with Edison. "Early on, I learned to trust your *instincts*. They're so...animal. Even the president was impressed by how you arrested that Venezuelan last week."

"I've got a feeling a big deal's about to go down," Edison said, turning a deaf ear to her flattery. "Can't you put Tom on this Selena Silverwood thing? Or Steve? Or Gary Hughes? Didn't Hughes crack the codes that exposed all the new military installations in Syria?"

"Gary's good," admitted Eleanor. "But you're better. And the president *was* impressed by the laptop case."

More like the lap*dog* case. While retrieving data from laptop computers stolen from overseas dignitaries, Edison had caught a Venezuelan official smuggling out information about American spies. When the man and his wife were nabbed, Edison wound up with the wife's dog.

"Did anyone adopt that puppy dog?" asked Eleanor.

"Puppy. Dog. I think that's redundant," remarked Edison.

Eleanor chose to ignore the grammar lesson. "Didn't you put an ad in the paper?"

"It appeared beside one of the suspicious classifieds I need to research," Edison lied, raking a hand through thick, tousled raven hair as he redirected the conversation. "And no. Nobody in their right mind would adopt that dog."

Eleanor softened. "How *is* Marshmallow?"

"Still alive. And I'm calling him M."

"Cute," returned Eleanor. "Like in the James Bond movies."

A sterling tag dangling from a scarlet collar had identified the dog, which looked like a four-pound marshmallow that had survived a whirlwind trip through a high-speed blender. At the Venezuelan dignitary's house, before coming home with Edison, the dog had licked Edison's face and cuddled. Since then he'd urinated on carpets, humped the leg of a Friday night date, gnawed Edison's favorite moccasins and exhibited dietary habits that excluded everything but filet mignon, cooked rare.

"Edison," Eleanor continued now, "we value your time and realize you require no supervision. You *are* your own boss here. However, CIIC alerted us to—"

"*CIIC* wants me to investigate Selena Silverwood?"

"As I said," Eleanor assured him, "we'd never waste your time."

"While at work, Ms. Silverwood's been writing in a personal diary that CIIC believes could be in code," added Newton. "She might be using the book to smuggle out information, which is why they need your input."

Carson tightened the knot of his tie, looking concerned. "What if this potential theft is related to those classified ads about bondage you mentioned?"

Against his better judgment, Edison got interested, rolled out a chair and seated himself. He glanced around the conference table. "Show me what you've got."

Edison noticed Eleanor tried not to look openly victorious as she reached toward a built-in console under the table and dimmed the overhead light. As a wall panel slid back to expose a screen, she lifted a remote control device and began clicking through a series of black-and-white slides, mostly still shots taken from video cameras hidden inside IBI.

"Selena Silverwood," she said. "Thirty years old. Class B security clearance. Employed eight months at IBI, and previously by civilian companies."

"You're kidding," Edison muttered, squinting at the screen. Any information he'd need would be in Selena Silverwood's file, right down to her bra and panty sizes, so he ignored Eleanor's ensuing monologue and attended to his personal impressions. And they *were* personal, he realized as a swift, unexpected pang claimed his groin. He quickly registered that she wasn't wearing a wedding ring, though he couldn't fathom why he cared, since he was used to the gorgeous, confident, manor-born types who liberally populated the Washington circuit.

Selena Silverwood was as tall as those women—at least five-ten—but the inward curve of her shoulders was calculated to hide her statuesque height, which meant long-boned limbs that could have made her as graceful as a panther seemed to hang from her frame like an oversize suit. She was definitely going out of her way not to be noticed, but was she a spy? Or simply lacking in self-confidence?

Edison shook his head, thinking she wouldn't be the first assistant to compensate for low wages by stealing. As another slow, inexplicable sensual tug morphed into a dull, heavy ache, he wondered if her hair was red or brown, and how she was really shaped under the loose, flowing dresses she favored. Maybe she intrigued him because she could easily look prettier than she did, he decided. But why didn't she try? And how would she act with a man? *Grateful for the attention,* he thought. She'd be easy on him if he was late, or forgot to call, or wasn't johnny-on-the-spot when it came to sending flowers—something that brought out Edison's protective instincts. He could easily imagine her being taken in by the kind of guy who took advantage, and there was something so damn vulnerable about her....

"Eleanor, get serious," he forced himself to say, cutting off his thoughts and tearing his eyes from Selena's picture. "She's a natural-born wallflower. She doesn't look even vaguely criminal."

"You've been fooled before," his boss reminded him.

"Not often." But Eleanor was right. Besides, CIIC never concerned itself with the innocent, and Edison hated traitors. Whoever his parents were, they'd abandoned him. Uncle Sam had kept him clothed and fed, and when Edison had shown talents, he'd been educated and given a job. *This* job. Which meant if the government wanted Selena Silverwood put under surveillance, Edison would gladly oblige.

"We want her checked out," Eleanor said. "Thoroughly."

From the looks of it, Selena Silverwood didn't get *thoroughly* very often—a thought that was still arousing his curiosity and quickening his blood. "I'll do my best."

"She's here in the IBI. complex. Building Five."

"Fourth floor," Newton added. "Sensitive Data Entry. You'll be her temporary assistant."

Edison groaned. "This is an undercover job? My typing's hunt and peck at best."

"You type ninety," corrected Eleanor. "Without error."

"A man's hard-won skills are supposed to be celebrated, not used against him," Edison said defensively. "Five minutes ago, I was investigating those classifieds. Now I'm demoted to typist."

Eleanor passed him a black-bound book. "You'll live."

"It's a copy of her diary," Carson explained. "She left the original in her desk drawer one night, and it was typed and bound for your convenience."

Edison frowned. "I work from originals. I can tell a lot from her handwriting." *Or from sleeping with her.* As he pushed aside the intrusive, if pleasant, thought, Eleanor plunged into the reasons the diary had been copied, not photographed, none of which made sense to Edison. Glancing down at the book, he wondered about the contents. Probably the usual—crushes on unattainable bosses, nights playing board games with the girls. If the woman had a boyfriend, he'd be an accountant or a stockbroker. Something safe and steady. Definitely not a spy.

Stifling a yawn over the anticipated boredom, Edison fixed his gaze on Selena Silverwood's picture again. She was exiting Building Five through automatic glass doors, swinging her hair over a shoulder and peering at a security camera through oversize rectangular glasses. She was hugging the original diary—a dainty, letter-size book—to a chest swallowed by a bulky blazer. Given the fact that this was his job, Edison was definitely more curious about that chest than he should have been. "She works in Building Five," he suddenly said. "What if she recognizes me? Knows I'm a code cracker?"

"Unlikely," countered Eleanor. "You've been working out of the country most of the time she's been with IBI. Besides, if she's seen you around the IBI complex, she'll think you're what you say you are—one of our floating temporaries. And CIIC is adamant. I'm under time pressure from them." Eleanor paused significantly. "There could be a promotion."

Edison couldn't help but ask, "For whom?"

Eleanor sighed. "You. But only if you watch this woman closely. See if she behaves suspiciously, in a way we haven't noticed on the cameras. And, of course, decipher her diary, if it's in code."

Big if. He'd have to research and analyze those classified ads on his own time, since, obviously, no one around here cared about catching real criminals. It was nearly impossible to imagine Selena Silverwood smuggling sensitive information out of the office, but she did bother him. As a woman. Glancing at the boss he'd been foolish enough to sleep with years ago, Edison reminded himself to maintain objectivity. He'd just have to ignore how his latest research subject had already gotten under his skin and into his blood.

OBJECTIVITY WAS impossible, Edison admitted an hour later, putting down his briefcase, his eyes riveting where the hem of a silk, navy-and-tan-checked dress swirled against Selena's delicate ankles. Looking unsettled by the curious male attention Edison wasn't bothering to hide, she leaned against a copy machine in the hallway and said, "Well, I believe I've shown you everything, Mr. Lone."

Not everything. One look and he'd felt sure there was more to her than met the eye. Oh, she probably wasn't a spy—he figured CIIC had just gotten overly cautious—but she was even more intriguing in the flesh. He just wished the black-and-white slides had provided some warning about how the low, honeyed quality of her voice would affect his heartbeat. A slow, suggestive smile curled his lips. "Shown me—" he arched an eyebrow "—everything?"

"Well..." Remarkable eyes that were outlined by unattractive, bookish, black-framed glasses drifted over him, as if drawn downward against their will, compelled to survey the fit of his tan slacks and black V-neck sweater. When those eyes found his again, they glinted darkly as if she were steeling herself against him, determined to ignore his flirtation at all costs. Before he could ask why, she continued, "Well, I've shown you the coffee machine and your personal shelf in the refrigerator. And—" Now she patted the copy machine lid affectionately "—our copier. After you've read the employee manual for our division, you'll want to further familiarize yourself with this machine. Because people call from all over the world for copies, our billing system's a little complex...."

What was complex was his reaction to this woman. As it turned out, she had skin that flushed the color of dusky-orange roses; hair that was probably technically termed auburn—pure autumn, all glorious golden sunbeams shooting through dark-brown chestnuts and rust-red leaves. Steady topaz eyes peered from behind those ugly glasses he was itching to remove. She had charm, intelligence and a compelling gangly grace, as if she'd recently experienced an unwanted growth spurt and hadn't quite caught up to it yet.

Realizing his eyes had settled once more where the dress brushed her ankles, Edison lifted his gaze, his body tightening when he noted how the silk brushed—and revealed—other parts of her: full sloping breasts, a nipped waist and lush backside. Just like color, movement did wonders. Still photographs hadn't captured the roll of her hips, the gentle sway of her breasts.

"Any questions about the copier?" When he didn't

answer immediately, she squinted, raising eyebrows the same autumnal color as her thick, shoulder-length hair. "Mr. Lone?"

"Uh, no. Copier seems fine." He smiled. "You, however, are an original, Selena." Before she could respond, he absently murmured in afterthought, "Selena. Pretty name. And please call me Edison."

She shot him a glance of censure that was one part surprised annoyance, two parts female pleasure, and then her gaze softened as if she'd finally decided he might be worthy of consideration. "Original?" She tossed the word over her shoulder as she motioned for him to follow her down the hallway. "You don't even know me." After a pause, she added, "Edison."

Enjoying the slow, easy sway of her backside, he murmured, "I'm beginning to think I'd like to."

Blowing out a soft, disapproving sigh, she led him into an open-concept work area. Floor-to-ceiling windows lined the perimeter, encasing forty or so identical glassed-in cubicles, the partitions of which muted sounds of humming printers and swiftly clicking computer keys. "Cozy," he pronounced dryly.

She shrugged. "Martha Stewart wasn't available."

"This office looks like it was decorated by The Terminator."

"Futuristic," she agreed, then pointed. "Voilà. Welcome to your work station."

A shiny steel desk topped by a computer, faced an identical computer on an identical shiny steel desk. He motioned a thumb toward the other computer. "And that?"

"Is my work space."

"So..." Seating himself in the regulation chair provided, he set his briefcase beside the desk and shot her a playful glance, realizing that somewhere during the introductions, he'd decided to seduce the truth out of her. The woman couldn't be a spy. No way. "This could get dangerous," he began. "Am I really supposed to face you all day, with nothing between us but a thin partition of glass?"

"Plexiglas," she corrected mildly, circling it. "And don't get any ideas. Big Brother is always watching."

"Ah..." His throat went dry as he surveyed her. "You have a sense of humor."

"Don't tell anyone." Her lip-glossed mouth suddenly came to life, twitching with amusement, making him realize how unusually full it was, how kissable. "As you know," she continued, "everything here at IBI is top secret."

He raised a dark eyebrow. "You included?"

She shrugged, the lift of her inward-curving shoulders correcting her posture, making him notice the enticing tilt of her breasts once again. "Of course. I wouldn't want to feel left out."

For a second, he almost forgot she was a suspect he'd been sent to investigate. "I'd ask you on a date," he said, surprised by and enjoying their banter, "but I'm afraid we're being taped."

"And photographed." Selena nodded easily at a ceiling-mounted camera. "Say cheese."

"Cheese," he repeated, wishing she wasn't quite so obviously aware of IBI's security system. Playing the part of a temporary worker, he added, "The last division where I was sent had cameras everywhere. Do you mind being watched all day?"

Her alluring eyes suddenly seemed too sharp, too intelligent. She surveyed him a long moment, then finally shrugged. "Depends who's doing the watching."

Everything about her bespoke the tension of contradictions, he decided. She wasn't noticeably pretty, but she was sexy as hell. Her eyes had remained unconsciously seductive, even as her obviously intelligent mind assessed him. He said, "What if *I'm* doing the watching?"

She smirked, those tantalizing lips twisting again, almost petulantly. "Then cameras would make me feel safer."

"You don't like men to provide your feelings of safety?"

"Men are hardly safe," she retorted. In the wake of a revealing blush that followed, she quickly added, "What? Do women always ask you to play the role of Great Protector?"

"Do you distrust men in general," he pressed trying not to sound too curious, "or did some specific male hurt you?"

Now she didn't look the least perturbed. "I asked first."

"Do woman ask me to protect them?" he repeated. "Never. I think they find me too dangerous."

"Or commitment shy."

Hearing the truth from her tasty-looking lips was more annoying than it should have been. This was supposed to be his game. His turf. His rules. He was here to watch her, and decipher her diary, which he felt more sure than ever wasn't in secret code. He fought the urge to tell her their sparring was getting a little too personal. Mostly because he had a suspicion that everything about him and Selena Silverwood was about to get personal. "I commit to plenty of things," he said, running a palm over his jet hair, loosening the waves as he brushed them back. "I've made a fledgling commitment to a dog named M, for instance."

The truth was, he'd never stayed with a woman longer than six months. That was his rule of thumb. *Leave them before they leave you.* Suddenly feeling edgy, Edison considered telling Eleanor she'd have to send down one of the other guys. Tom. Steve. Gary Hughes. Anybody. Selena Silverwood was going to be a royal pain in the butt. In her pictures, she'd looked unattractive. In person, she was more physically alluring than she knew. But her presumptive air was now threatening to bring out the worst in him. "You know so much about me," he continued, chiding. "What? Did somebody send over my dossier?"

When she grinned, now seemingly enjoying this, the way her face lit up made his heart stutter. "Does the idea make you nervous?" she teased. "What are you hiding? Six ex-wives? Arrests for unspeakable acts?"

"You've got a vivid imagination."

She released a soft, musical chuckle. "So I'm told."

His eyes fixed on hers. "I like imagination in a woman."

She surveyed him curiously. "Really?"

He nodded. "Yeah. I like a sharp tongue, too. Do you always flirt with temporaries?"

"Flirting?" Her voice turned mild. "Is that what I'm doing?"

"Definitely. And it's starting to sound like an invitation."

"Then I'd better quit. IBI might fire us."

His eyes lingered on her mouth a second too long, and in that second, he knew he'd happily take his pink slip if it meant heading for a bedroom with her. "If you need anything, let me know," she suddenly said. "And you really should read the employee manual. It's in the top, right-hand drawer of the desk. Our rules differ from other departments'."

"A man can't break rules unless he knows them," he conceded.

"I wouldn't know," she assured him. "I never break rules."

Raw lust made him want to believe it. He'd never fall for a traitor, which was what she'd be if her diary really was written in code. While she busied herself with work, he leaned down, drew the black-bound diary from his briefcase and surreptitiously inserted it between the open pages of the employee manual. Even if she noticed the book, she wouldn't recognize it as her own diary. Lifting both books to desk level, he tipped the cover of the manual in her direction. "The employee manual. Thanks for recommending it. It looks interesting."

She merely rolled eyes that glinted with amusement and began working again. Relaxing, Edison glanced down and realized the diary had a title: *Night Pleasures*. Not exactly what he'd expected. Frowning, he drew a sharp breath as his eye caught a sentence fragment in midparagraph: "...she panted softly, breathlessly, as she ran through the near dark." His body tensed. What was going on here? His heartbeat quickened as he scanned the rest of the page.

> ...her body ached, swelling with awareness and burning with fire as her eyes flitted over the floor-to-ceiling mirrored walls. Long-handled torches lined the smoky, scented passageway, and sensuous tongues of flame licked the mirrors. That same fire stroked inside her, but she knew the burning heat was nothing compared to what she'd experience when she felt the warm, sometimes gentle, hands of the man she sought, the Marquis de Lancroix.
>
> Where was he?
>
> She'd been in this otherworldly place for so long, suppressing shudders of anticipation, struggling for a glimpse of his long, wild raven mane and

sleek, muscled body. Worrying her lower lip between her teeth, she prayed her heart would stop racing, but it only beat faster, because she was about to be seduced in this pleasure palace. Only the wealthiest man in France could afford such a sensual private playhouse, with its maze of mirrored halls and air scented with incense....

She gasped. There he was! Pressing a hand to her heart, she whirled and stared into a room. But he'd vanished! What was happening? she wondered in confusion, her mind reeling. Was the marquis playing tricks on her? Had he drugged her with a potion at the masked ball? Was that why she felt so lost? So aroused? So disoriented?

And hadn't she just seen him? She could swear he'd been reflected in the mirrors in one of the rooms, reclining on a bed, everything about him bespeaking excess: his bold, unapologetic nakedness, the thrust of his sex, the fiery flames prancing on a body that looked like sculpted bronze. She spun around again. And again. She spun until she swore she saw him everywhere. Then she moved forward, inhaling sharply as she skated her fingertips along the mirrors.

"There!" Her voice suddenly hitched as she passed another room. "I've found you!" But when she reached out, her palm hit a mirror, and she found herself peering into yet another sensuous room, staring at where crystal-blue waters tumbled into a pool, gushing around the mural painted on the bottom. Her eyes became riveted on nude sea nymphs and mermaids pleasuring proudly aroused men, and she suddenly admitted she shouldn't have sneaked away from the ball to meet Lancroix. She'd allowed the marquis to love her body before now, of course, but never in his private playhouse made for sin. Tonight she'd lied to her mama and attendants, and now she'd be wise to find her way out of this place. A footstep sounded! Had Lancroix followed her, after all?

"Lancroix?"

She gasped, suddenly startled by her own reflection. Tugging the glittering silver mask from her dark eyes, she threw it to the stone floor. There. Let him find her clothes scattered in the hallway. It would serve him right for not meeting her as he'd promised. Yes, she should leave. He'd find scraps of costume—the chain around her waist, her mask. He'd be so frustrated, filled with want for a naked woman—for her—but she'd be gone.

And yet it was a shame. She *had* dressed for him tonight—in sensual, near-transparent silver silk scarves that draped over her breasts and lower body, but left her belly bare. She'd already felt his hands...already knew that a flick of his practiced wrist could send the fabric flying. "Marquis de Lancroix?" she called abruptly. "Is that you, sir?"

She never knew, because the man came too quickly, grabbing her from behind, his strong arms seizing her waist without warning. The hard, heated impact of his naked body took her breath away, just as a wind gusted down the passageway, extinguishing the torches.

His breath came then, warm on her cheeks, his low, seductive growl eliciting shivers from the deepest recesses of her being. "Lover," he whispered.

The word she'd hoped to hear from Lancroix warmed her, but did the rough stubble teasing her neck really belong to the marquis? Were these his bare thighs, braced against the backs of hers? In the darkness, an eye mask grazed her cheek, which meant that whoever he was, he'd come from the ball.

"Who are you?" she croaked.

"The man who's been lusting for you."

"You don't even know me."

"But I do, Mademoiselle Duclaire."

He knew her name! Before she could decide whether or not to struggle, he was dragging her backward, the strength of his embrace so sensually possessive that her knees buckled. "Sir, I demand you identify yourself!" she managed to exclaim as bold hands slid upward—tracing her bare ribs, then suddenly, swiftly, curling over her breasts in a first touch that left her reeling and took her breath. Her heart beat out of control. The man definitely knew what he was doing.

His voice was as dangerously silky as the hands that cupped and squeezed. "I'll make the demands."

"Lancroix?" she murmured faintly. "Is that you?" Or was her body aching for a stranger?

"Do you really care?"

No, she admitted to herself, not when his mouth descended with the verve of a savage. His tongue plunged, driving silkenly inside her mouth as surely as a warrior's lance, while magic fingers began stroking her peaking nipples. She knew it was Lancroix—it had to be—and with his every touch, she realized she loved him. As fiery hands melted away her costume, making every erogenous inch of her burn, she knew she'd give this man anything.

"Ah..." he murmured, dropping scalding kisses along her neck as he dispensed with her skirt and slid a finger between her buttocks, gently lifting the strap of the thong. "Nice, Mademoiselle Duclaire. Very nice."

A cry was torn from her as he continued tugging the leather, slowly working the strap, making it pull in front until she squirmed, about to burst. Vaguely, sucking a breath between her teeth, she wondered how he'd undressed her so quickly. "Yes," she whispered simply, nonsensically, her heart hammering as she felt his hard length graze her flesh. "Yes." There was simply no other word she could offer him....

"It's good you don't intend to fight me," he stated, the urgency in his words as seductive as his body. "It's no use."

And he was right, she realized as he toyed with the waist chain she wore, suddenly tightening it, making her skin quiver and her nerves dance. "Nice," he murmured throatily. "So very nice." Silken chest hairs flattened against her back as he embraced her more tightly from behind, holding her to the hard, muscled wall of his chest, his palms thrusting upward once more, lifting her breasts, holding them high as if he were making an offering to a goddess.

"Bring the salts," she whispered, feeling the lights in her mind extinguishing as she arched against him, pleasure arrowing to the juncture of her thighs. "I'm going to faint."

"You will," he promised, cupping where she felt so swollen. "From the pleasure."

And then he turned her head, kissing her until everything inside her became as darkly sensuous as the mirrored passageway, as liquid and hot as the summer night. Thumbs and fingers teased her taut nipples, roughening and pinching, making her whimper from the torment. "Good," he praised softly as she writhed.

"Please," she whispered back, her jagged breaths bringing in scents of his skin that made her head swim. Groaning, he twisted his hips, swiftly lowering her to the floor. She shivered as he lay on top of her, his naked body covering hers—toe to toe, chest to chest. Nipples brushed. Lips brushed.

Palms brushed. It was all too good to be true, she thought, feeling his muscles tense. His soft, panting breath stirred her hair as he claimed her with a piercing thrust. She gasped. It was deep, so deep it would have hurt—maybe even killed her—if not for the unbelievable pleasure....

Edison started. *What the hell?* he thought, his mind reeling back to the present. Suddenly he was staring, slack-jawed, into eyes that looked less like topazes now and more like fire-warmed whiskey. With a rush of awareness, he registered that his whole body was hot, his mind still full of pure, unadulterated sex. Was this some sort of practical joke? Had Eleanor roped him into this, knowing Selena's diary wasn't in secret code?

"Did you say something?" he managed to ask.

Selena was frowning as if she were an entomologist and he were a new species of insect. "You're really devouring that employee manual," she said curiously.

He wanted—no, needed—to devour *her*. He was fit to be tied—literally. Preferably with the silver scarves that had barely covered Mademoiselle Duclaire. Drawing a deep breath, he licked his dry lips.

"If you're thirsty," she said, watching him, "the water fountain's right next to the elevator."

He could hardly leave the desk at the moment, given how her diary had affected him. "Thanks, but I'll keep reading."

She squinted. "That interesting, huh?"

"Employee manuals. Nothing like them," he forced

himself to say. "Racy," he couldn't help but add. "Satisfying."

Her tone was dry. "You must lead a truly exciting life."

It had gotten a lot more exciting as he'd read *Night Pleasures.* But none of this made sense. Had someone wanted to distract him from researching the classified ads? This diary had to be just that: a diary. If it was in code, it would have been predictable, written only for show. But this was full of heart, full of longing....

Selena was still frowning at the cover of the employee manual. "Are you really going to read that again?"

Edison glanced down, his eyes catching the words *pure velvet magic slid inside her.* "A real page turner," he assured.

"I'm beginning to think you're a little strange."

He eyed her. "Do you want to find out the truth?"

"You sound so mysterious. Are you sure you're not a spy?"

"No. But maybe you are. Is Selena even your real name?"

"Yes. But my parents almost named me Silence."

Surely she wouldn't banter like this if she really was stealing IBI secrets. "Silence?"

She nodded. "I was a seventies baby. Hippie parents."

"Funny," he said. "You look normal enough."

"I rebelled."

Judging from her diary, she was quite the free spirit. Edison took another deep breath, reminding himself that even if she wasn't spying, indulging fantasies while on IBI's payroll wasn't exactly kosher. When he was at work, he did what they paid him for: work. "Rebelled?" he couldn't help but say. "Does this mean you've got something against free love?"

She considered. "Love never comes without a price."

"What price are you willing to pay for it, Selena?"

The words had simply slipped out, and now her whiskey-colored eyes darkened as if the conversation had turned too heavy. He was aware once more of the effect her fantasies had on his body. "I'd rather be alone," she finally said, "than pay a price for love."

"My feeling exactly," he admitted. But that hardly barred him from playing the Marquis de Lancroix to her Mademoiselle Duclaire. "So, you like to be alone? Does that mean forever, or just tonight?"

Faint color had risen in her cheeks, and he could see her throat work as she swallowed. "You ask a lot of questions."

"Mind if I ask one more?"

Crossing her arms over her ample chest, she glanced away, drolly rolling her eyes. "Could I stop you?"

"No. What about dinner?"

Her eyes darted to his again, and she smiled. "What about it?"

He sent her a long, sideways glance. "Do you want to eat it?"

"I usually do."

"With me?"

Her eyes narrowed. "Ah. Let me guess. You know a

quaint little Italian place with small, round, candlelit tables and a cellarful of dusty wine bottles."

She'd hit the nail on the head. The place was called Antonio's. But because he'd just read her diary, Edison couldn't help but say, "Actually, for you, Selena, I was thinking about something French. Passer la Nuit."

"Given how diligently you were reading the employee manual, I figured you were the conscientious type," she countered. "Doesn't it bother you that we work together?"

He shrugged. "I'm only a temporary."

She considered so long that he almost withdrew the offer, but then she simply said, "Okay."

He tried to hide his surprise. "What about seven o'clock? I'll pick you up."

"Seven-thirty," she countered. "I'll drive my own car and meet you at the restaurant."

Given her fantasies, he could see why she'd want some control of the situation. No telling what might happen if she let herself go. Now that he'd read part of her diary, he was well aware that she was a lust machine, and yet she'd seemed so oddly vulnerable and straight-laced. Was she really inexperienced? Were these fantasies merely her way of trying on the role of seductress? "Seven-thirty," he found himself murmuring. "At Passer la Nuit."

"Looking forward to it."

Lowering his head, he pretended to read. Did she have a lot of experience with men, or just an imagination as vivid as Technicolor? he wondered once more.

And was she stealing from IBI? Was this diary actually in code?

Flipping through the pages, he bit back a soft groan as he read, "Every inch of him went taut. He was ready to explode, but he wanted to hold back—*had* to hold back. He was waiting for his soft, untutored butterfly, whose wings were about to unfold."

If he didn't stop reading, Selena Silverwood would be lucky to make it through an appetizer tonight—Italian, French or otherwise. But then, a job was a job. And because he was a patriot, he was duty-bound to continue mulling over every steamy word she'd written. *For God and country,* he thought dryly, bracing himself against the soft, feminine scent of her that drifted over the glass partition.

And then, lowering his head, he immersed himself in *Night Pleasures.*

2

"I'M GOING TO BE LATE," Selena muttered, her belly fluttering in anticipation. No doubt Edison Lone was already waiting for her at a secluded, candlelit table at the restaurant.

"Passer la Nuit," she huffed, shaking her head. Spend the Night. She should have known he'd suggest the most romantic, airy French restaurant in town, not to mention the most expensive. His reputation had preceded him. God only knew how many women he'd seduced over Passer la Nuit's best Dijon filet and a few heady goblets of burgundy.

"You can't say you weren't warned," she whispered. But she hated playing the role of ugly duckling. She simply couldn't bring herself to continue doing so tonight. She'd hated the way he'd sized her up today, those liquid blue eyes softening in what she took to be sympathy, as if she were still fat, friendless and ugly, the daughter of overly educated, back-to-the-earth liberals who were determined to make a life where they didn't belong, in the country. Not about to dwell on the devastation of her high school years, or how hard she'd worked to change herself, she sighed. *Forget it.* She'd long ago proved she could be every bit as dangerous as the kids who'd hurt her.

In the closet, her hand skated over the loose, ankle-length dresses she usually wore to IBI, then settled where it shouldn't have—on a shimmering silver dress procured for her parents' last wedding anniversary. It was right out of her fantasies. Sumptuous, barely-there crepe was sexily torn in tatters around the shoulders and draped into a sheath with a jagged hem. The matching three-inch heels would bring her eye level with Edison.

"And you'll need every extra inch of leverage," she told herself, imagining his tall, lanky body and the thick, touchable, raven hair that brushed his shoulders. Slipping the dress from its black velvet hanger, she sighed as the fabric teased her fingertips.

"If I wear this," she murmured, "it'll be proof I've lost my mind." She couldn't afford to attract a man at the moment, least of all Edison Lone. Besides, the best men were those she conjured in her imagination. Real men meant trouble.

"Why didn't I just say no to dinner?" she admonished herself in a rush of panic. Should she back out? Stand him up? But how could she, when she had to find out what he was doing working in Sensitive Data Entry?

Shimmying, she let the towel wrapped around her naked body drop to the floor. Soft scents left by perfumed bathwater rose from her skin. She wondered if Edison would notice the sweet fragrance.

Heat seeped into her cheeks. She was being a fool. Reflected in a full-length mirror on the closet door, she took in the beige carpet behind her, the muted earth-tone bedspread and bare white walls. The apartment had all the charm of a low-budget motel. The black-framed glasses on the nightstand had plastic, nonprescription lenses. Most of the clothes in the closet weren't to her taste. Only the open diary on the desk hinted at her real personality. Ever since an editor had contacted her about publishing the fantasies, the diary had become a good luck charm. It was her ticket out of Washington. One more way to generate the money she needed to escape...

Otherwise, the room looked exactly like what it was: a place she didn't intend to live in long. Within weeks, she'd be gone, she figured. And there'd be no trace of Selena Silverwood.

Silverwood wasn't her real name, anyway.

"So don't get confused about what you're doing at IBI," she lectured herself softly. "Or with Edison Lone." He might be the most appealing man she'd ever laid eyes on, but this was a job, and she needed to know why he'd suddenly shown up, seated at a desk across from her.

"A floating temp," she muttered, shaking her head. Even if she hadn't read his dossier, she'd know better. Not that his name, rank and serial number had prepared her for the reality. When he'd stood next to her, his shoulders had seemed broader than she'd anticipated, the scent and warmth coming from his body infinitely more bothersome. She'd expected something else from the orphan who'd made good. A cold, calloused man, she supposed. With a chip on his shoulder. Instead, despite his self-contained watchfulness, he looked like he had a heart. Not to mention royal-blue eyes so searching that gazing into them had aroused guilt feelings she hadn't guessed she had.

Had he been sent to spy on her? Was she about to get caught? Or had he come to Sensitive Data Entry for reasons having nothing to do with her? She thought of how the flourescent lights had made his jet hair shine where it curled around his ears, and about how those shocking blue eyes glowed like lasers in a face tanned the color of toasted nuts. And then her eyes settled once more on her diary. If the Marquis de Lancroix could leap from the pages, he'd look more or less like Edison.

Slowly, she unzipped and stepped into the silver dress, trying not to imagine the look on Edison's face when she'd glide into Passer la Nuit, trailing perfume. Instead of truffles and tortes for dessert, she hoped he'd be eating out of the palm of her hand.

After that, who knew? The truth was, she'd run from men all her life—with just cause. She always tried to tell herself she didn't care, that sex was overrated and that, when it came to excitement, no man could compete with her work.

But she was thirty now, and defenses she'd erected against love were crumbling. Once red and raw, past scars were losing themselves to memory, their traces barely visible anymore, not to herself or others. She'd worked damn hard at making those old wounds heal, and exploring her innermost dreams of sensual pleasure had been a big part of that. But was she ready to make fantasies a reality?

Maybe. What used to feel like career excitement had started seeming more like plain, old, everyday danger. Earlier this year, Bruce Levinson had gotten killed, doing exactly what she was at IBI. Not that she could back out now. She'd have to play the game, try not to get caught, and figure out where Edison Lone fit into the picture.

"A floating temp," she murmured again. "Yeah, right."

She'd been so sure she'd played the unattractive secretary to perfection. The role, she thought with a rush of anger, came easily enough. But now it seemed as if someone was onto her. Were they? Had Edison been sent to scrutinize her files? Rifle through her desk drawers? Was she in danger?

"Definitely," she decided aloud, thinking of how he'd tied her insides into knots. She'd never flirted with a man so easily as she'd flirted with him today. Reaching behind her, she zipped up the dress, then slid stockinged feet into shimmering silver shoes. Studying herself dispassionately, she found wistful emotion twisting unexpectedly inside her. Why couldn't she be a million miles from here? Somewhere without secrets, lies and hidden agendas? Someplace where a man like Edison Lone really could become her lover? Under the circumstances, using him to test out her fantasies seemed seriously unadvisable....

"Too bad," she whispered. Regardless of his unsuitability as her first lover, she wasn't about to let him think she was a geek. Nervously arranging a scrap of silver fabric against her collarbone, she took a deep breath. Dammit, why did she have to be so desperately attracted to the man most likely to interfere with her subterfuge at IBI?

THERE WAS SOMETHING dreamy in the air, something almost magical, and when Selena breezed into Passer la Nuit dressed almost like the woman in her diary, Edison was lost. Seeing a body she never should have kept hidden, draped with what looked to be silver scarves, he no longer cared if she was stealing from IBI. He was taking Selena Silverwood to bed. Tonight.

Every time he looked at her, he found himself thinking of her diary, of love scenes in shallow pools and between masked partners in dark, scented, mirrored passageways. He half wished he hadn't tortured himself by reading until he'd left his house to meet her, since the diary had filled him with expectations for the evening. Now they'd finished eating, and he nodded toward the lace-veiled French doors. "Ready to go?"

Offering the slightest lift of a bare shoulder, she drew a sip of burgundy through wine-reddened lips. The flame from a candle at the cozy table made her eyes look like pools of aged whiskey, and made him think that the black-framed glasses she usually wore were a definite mistake. Without them, and in this dress, she was stunning. "I'm enjoying it here," she murmured.

And he was enjoying watching the thin, scarcely noticeable silver glitter play on her eyelids whenever she glanced at him. As she did so now, something—warmth from her amber gaze or from his own brandy-laced coffee—slid through his bones, turning his voice husky. "I thought you'd like this place, Selena."

"I do," she said simply. "I'm glad we came."

"Me, too."

Catching her fingers lazily between his, Edison marveled at the spark of electricity that jumped between them. Like her seductively tilted eyes, it reminded him that dinner was only one of the reasons he'd brought her here. Espionage was another. So was sex. He was practiced with women, but he hadn't expected the shock he'd experienced seeing her in a cocktail dress. He glided his fingers along her hand, then rubbed the hollow of her wrist with the pad of his thumbs. "Your pulse is racing."

She eyed him. "Really?"

"Really," he assured her, feeling as drugged as the woman in her diary, as if he'd taken a potion. She ran her gaze over him, letting it settle on his deep blue, V-necked sweater. A gift from an ex-girlfriend, the sweater matched his eyes, complemented his finely woven gray slacks and revealed a hint of swirling dark chest hair that itched for her caress.

Her voice matched his for throatiness, as if she, too,

had been sated by the heavy French meal. "You have excellent taste in restaurants, Edison Lone."

"Women, too."

Chuckling softly at the compliment, she glanced away, her face a study in contrasts: pleasure, embarrassment, confusion. "So," she began abruptly, "you work at IBI part-time, and otherwise, you teach?"

His gaze hadn't left her face. "You won't get away with it."

Only the slight widening of her eyes gave away a startled response. "Get away with what?"

Gently pulling on her wrist, he drew her closer, wondering if she really did have something to hide. "With ignoring my flirtation. I am going to take you to bed, Selena."

"You're very direct," she said in a near whisper.

"Looking at you makes me feel I don't have time to lose." He shrugged. "Besides, I know what I want."

"And you take the quickest route to get it?" she asked breathlessly.

He wasn't the least bit offended. "Especially when I want it badly." Pausing, he added, "And I want you badly."

Recovering, she offered a slight smile. "Don't you believe in getting to know a person first?"

He laughed. "That's good."

She frowned. "What?"

"You're speaking of firsts. It implies I'll get seconds."

"Really," she chided. "Don't you get to know your dates?"

"You, yes," Edison said honestly. "But not every woman I take to bed."

Her glance was droll. "I never said we were going to bed."

The denial shouldn't have challenged him, but it did. He tried not to let it show. "You don't have to say it," he replied, his leisurely gaze studying her. "It's in your eyes...in the way you carry yourself." Pausing, he shook his head. Didn't she realize she was leaning seductively toward him, offering a tantalizing view of her ripe breasts? His eyes flickered possessively down, hot as the candle flame, and he savored a fantasy about how he'd circle a taut nipple with his tongue until she writhed from the pleasure. Oh, there were many things he had in mind for Selena. He was every bit as imaginative as the marquis. For now, he settled on lifting a finger and lightly tracing a bare shoulder. His voice was silky. "No woman trying to stay out of a man's bed wears a dress like this."

"You're very sure of your ability to get a woman into bed."

"It's what happens after she's in bed that interests me." Letting her mull over the comment, he sipped coffee that had come just the way he liked it—strong and black, splashed with top-shelf brandy. After a moment, he offered another careless smile. "Of course, if you need to talk first, we certainly can. Some women consider it foreplay."

Now her lips twitched with a smile. "How obliging."

He smiled back. "I can be much more obliging than that."

She took a sip of wine, then shrugged, the feigned nonchalance not reaching her eyes. "Tell me more about yourself."

"Like I said, I'm a teacher." The lie had rolled impulsively from his tongue, and tomorrow he'd have to cover his tracks, since she could expose him with one phone call. For now, the fib enabled him to share more of himself, something he'd discovered he wanted to do with Selena. "I only work for IBI when I'm not teaching," he added. "During spring breaks, like now, and in the summer. A friend told me I could sign up, get a security clearance."

"Data entry's odd work for an English teacher."

"Keeps me busy," he offered, shrugging easily, his eyes lowering appreciatively. Everything about her was making him ache: the candlelight shimmering on her bare shoulders, the intoxicating scent of wine coming in tandem with her breath. Reaching out, he adjusted a scrap of material on her shoulder again. "As delicate as a spider's web."

She smiled. "Afraid I'll snare you?"

"Afraid you won't," he corrected, flashing her another smile. He shrugged. "The money from IBI funds my hobby."

"Which is?"

"Cracking codes," he answered, thinking Selena was the puzzle he'd most like to crack. What had possessed her to write down such sensual fantasies? While he was sure they weren't in code, he figured it would be interesting to test the waters, to see if she reacted to knowing how he spent his time. "I often try to crack the codes to old manuscripts."

"You mean like the Rosetta stone?"

He nodded. "Right now, I'm working on what's called the Voynich manuscript. I'm interested in old cave drawings, too. On vacations, I go hunting for them."

"Like Indiana Jones?"

"More or less." His blood quickened at thoughts of his work, and at the answering excitement in her eyes. "Secretive communications of any kind draw me like a magnet. I've always been more interested in what people don't say than in what they do."

"Really?"

He nodded. "I get lost in word puzzles."

"When you want to crack a code, what do you do first?"

Her interest seemed genuine, and he figured she'd probably be defensive if she had something to hide. CIIC had to be wrong. She was on the level. "Check for substitution words and anagrams. Or for known codes people might use. Sometimes I look for pinpricks over words and letters, to see if a message can be pieced together by connecting the dots." His eyes settled once more on her bare shoulder. "And there are heat-sensitive codes."

Not missing the innuendo, she murmured, "Heat sensitive?"

He nodded again. "Not to mention secret inks."

At that, she looked genuinely delighted, and since countless women had had their eyes glaze over when he talked about work, or worse, been jealous of his passion for it, he felt encouraged, maybe more than he should have. "During the Second World War," he continued, leaning back and rifling a hand through his hair, "soldiers used invisible, heat-sensitive inks on eggshells. Later, the recipient would hard-boil the eggs and peel the shell."

"And the secret message would be written on the egg," she guessed with a soft laugh.

"Exactly."

"Tasty."

Not nearly as tasty as she looked. "A woman in Germany kept special inks stored in the dyes of her scarves."

Selena considered, then said, "So, why do you like cave drawings? What's the connection?"

"They tell stories."

Her eyes—rimmed by kohl pencil, the lashes darkened—drifted around the room, and her breasts rose with a deep breath as she took in the wall paintings—tasteful nudes in heavy gilt frames. "I suppose most pieces of art do tell stories."

"In that dress, you're a piece of art," he couldn't help but say, images from her diary playing once more in his head. "What story are you waiting to tell, Selena?"

When she shrugged, the dress slipped a fraction, revealing another inch of creamy skin, just the hint of a sloping breast. "I hardly think I'm like a cave drawing."

"I'm convinced you have the same innocence," he murmured. No way in hell was she guilty of wrongdoing. She was sexy, yes. But involved in espionage? Never. Given a few more days, he'd prove it, too.

She was squinting. "How can cave drawings be innocent?"

"Easy. They look untutored. Primitive. And they possess a raw passion characteristic of the ancients."

Another smile tilted her mouth. "Just the ancients, huh?"

"Oh, don't worry, there's plenty of passion to be had in the present," he assured her with a laugh. "But not if we stay here all night."

He could see her throat work. "I should get home."

"You will," he promised, capturing her hand as he rose. "Eventually."

She gazed up at him. "I meant sooner than eventually."

As she stood, he draped her shawl around her shoulders. Loosely woven silver threads brushed his fingertips, leaving him to imagine how soft her naked skin would feel gliding beneath his palms. Placing a hand under her elbow, he guided her to the street, and when her body grazed his, he tried not to notice they were a perfect fit. She was eye level, too. He liked that.

They'd walked a half block when she nodded. "My car."

"Sure you won't come to my place? Meet M?"

The dog's name was so foolish that mention of it broke the dreamy mood. Her laughter was like bubbles, and she was clearly thinking of a point earlier in the evening when he'd amused her with stories about the dog's exploits. "I'm afraid of what M would do to me."

Edison smiled. "You should be. I'm running ads in three more newspapers now."

"Still no takers?"

"No one's that masochistic."

She merely laughed. "You're going to wind up keeping him."

She was right, of course. And standing with her on the crowded sidewalk, in the moonlight, on a perfect spring night, Edison felt better than he had in a long time. There was something else he hadn't anticipated: that, quite simply, he'd be so smitten with Selena Silverwood. As she leaned against the door of her car, his eyes captured hers again. Surely she wasn't planning to deny the energy coursing between them and go home? "So, you really think I'll wind up with M?"

"I've got a sixth sense about these things."

"Sure you didn't read my dossier?"

"You keep asking me that."

And maybe with cause. For the briefest second, Edison could swear fear and guilt flashed in her eyes. But under the streetlamps, it was too dark to read something as complex as emotions in a woman's eyes. Still, what if she *was* stealing secrets? What if what was between them was wiping out his common sense?

He glanced at her car. Nothing flashy, just a black

compact. If she was ripping off IBI, she wasn't spending the money. When he'd checked to see if her bank balance was in line with her salary, he'd found it was.

Taking a step, he glided his hands under the shawl and up her arms until he was cupping bare shoulders. Slowly, he rubbed deep circles with his thumbs, heat from the touch jolting him. Leaning forward, so she'd feel his breath on her cheek, he huskily whispered, "Going home's a mistake."

She eased back a fraction. "Why?"

Maybe she was looking for reassurances about how much he'd enjoyed dinner and her company. Instead of giving them, he ran a finger under the shoulder strap of her dress and said, "Because you came here in a dress that looks like I've already torn it off you." And because, despite his niggling doubts, the CIIC and Eleanor had gotten her all wrong. Selena Silverwood was innocent.

She was also fascinating. Outwardly shy, she was inwardly on fire with fantasies, and he wanted her.

She was smiling. "A man has his limits, huh?"

"You're definitely pushing my envelope." He'd prove her innocent, too. As soon as he could, he'd break into her apartment and get the original diary. As he'd told Eleanor, handwriting was very revealing, and Selena's would tell him everything he needed to know.

As he brought their bodies flush, unseen bands tightened around his chest. He registered the tension in her thighs, a quiver of muscle and female heat, and when she shivered, he knew damn well it had nothing to do with the spring chill. Brushing a tendril of autumnal hair from her cheek, he realized that it, just like the shawl and her skin, was silken beyond belief. "You look undecided, Selena."

"I didn't know there was a decision to be made."

"Sure is."

She arched an eyebrow. "About?"

"About how you want this night to end." At the sudden slight stiffening of her body, he felt more sure than ever that the guys at CIIC had gone crazy. Selena was vibrating with a need she was desperately trying to hold back. "Are you concerned because we're coworkers?"

She shrugged. "I'm not sure what I feel," she said honestly.

Tilting his chin, he lowered his head and angled his lips so they hovered over hers. "Why don't I decide for you?" he murmured. And then he simply covered her mouth with his. The pressure was slow and sweet, his tongue warm and probing. He'd meant it to be a gentleman's first brief kiss, but need hit him hard, slamming into him with a swift punch as her soft breasts pressed against the wall of his chest. He felt the tips tighten, the sudden flutter of her heart.

"What are you doing to me?" he whispered, cradling her hips to his so she could feel how badly he needed her. Against her mouth, still savoring her taste, he raggedly added, "Home. Come home with me, Selena."

To his surprise, she whispered, "Yes."

3

SHE NEVER SHOULD HAVE gone to his house, Selena thought the next day as she secured a file under her arm and headed for the copy machine, trying to ignore the fact that Edison was behind her, the brush of his hand-stitched Italian loafers sounding soft against the gray carpet.

His voice was equally soft. "Selena. Wait."

Wait. Such an inconsequential word shouldn't have evoked a response, but she'd waited all her life to have dinner in a restaurant such as Passer la Nuit with a man like Edison Lone. He was brilliant. Funny. Sexy. And he kissed in a way a woman apparently couldn't recover from. Feeling self-conscious, she tried to ignore that she'd left her black-framed glasses at home this morning and spritzed on perfume.

This was no time to get acquainted with Edison. For all she knew, the two of them would meet again down the road—possibly in criminal court. She'd been functioning on knee-jerk attraction, but now she had to concentrate on why she'd come to IBI—to gather information. During dinner, she'd become convinced that Edison hadn't been sent to spy on her, which was all she needed to know.

"Selena."

Taking a deep breath, she stopped in her tracks, waited a second, then turned around. "Look," she managed to say, her throat constricting with unwanted emotion as their eyes locked. "I meant what I said, Edison."

"What you said *when?*" He shot an annoyed glance toward a black video camera as if he'd like nothing more than to rip it from the wall. She knew Eleanor Luders was his supervisor, but who else was he reporting to? Newton Finch? Carson Cumberland? If he'd been sent to spy on her, which Selena now doubted, he wouldn't want his superiors to know he'd tried to seduce her, would he? He'd nearly succeeded, too, she acknowledged, warmth coursing through her veins.

"When?" he demanded again. "When we were having dinner last night? Or when you kissed me?"

"When you kissed *me,*" she corrected petulantly.

"And not for the last time."

"Really?" she couldn't help but retort mildly. The wounds from her past were surfacing, and with them, the need to both challenge him and distance herself from him.

He leveled a long stare at her, then flicked his eyes down to her mouth with a hunger he didn't bother to hide. "You're hard on men, aren't you?"

"Not intentionally."

"Seems to me like you're working at it, in my case."

"Then I guess we have a difference of opinion," she replied, resenting the audible catch in her breath and her shiver of excitement. Rejecting him wasn't easy when she felt trapped by his dark-as-midnight stare. Or when another of the cloud-soft, brushed-cotton sweaters he wore—this one cream colored—revealed a sprinkling pelt of wild, touchable chest hair. Or when tailored khaki slacks hugged hips that had cradled her own last night. Inadvertently, her gaze dipped to the bold, curved outline of his unmistakably male contours, bringing a rush of warmth to her skin.

"What you said *when?*" Edison repeated, his tone lowering seductively, the sudden, unexpected gentleness of the demand doing nothing to ameliorate the grim line of his mouth.

She lifted her gaze to his. She'd been staring at him so hard that, for a full second, she had no idea what he was talking about. "After," she managed to answer. She'd meant to say "after dinner," but only the first word made it from her lips.

"After." He echoed the word like a curse. "You mean, after you came to my house, got scared, then turned around and ran home like a scared rabbit?"

"Not exactly how I'd put it."

"No, I don't suppose you would." He was assessing every inch of her—from the emerald tank top she wore under a bulky black blazer, to the silk wrap skirt grazing her ankles—and she felt sure he was considering the slow removal of each article. Heaven help her, but she wanted to feel fabric falling from her skin: the tank top, skirt, panties...everything. She braced herself against the unwanted, traitorous response of her own body, but her belly tightened, her knees weakened and, worst of all, her breasts strained, beading under the tank top. Awareness sharpened the eyes that studied her. The man didn't miss a thing.

"We work together, Edison," she forced herself to say, surprised by how calm she sounded. "And last night...uh, at Passer la Nuit, I realized I made a mistake."

"What happened last night was no mistake."

"I just said it was."

"That's the thing about disagreements," he said, his voice dropping to little more than a murmur. "In the heat of the moment, they can get so interesting." He edged nearer, his dark eyes possessive, the pure romance of the restaurant coming back to her as he did. Heavy lace, she thought, fighting the sudden buckling of her knees. Starburst candles. Male appreciation in mesmerizing eyes.

With a sudden, audible inhalation, she drew in a man-in-the-woods cologne that made her mind reel as the scent flowed into her blood, electrifying it, making it dance. Fighting the feelings, she said, "We're in the office, in case you haven't noticed."

"I noticed." His unnerving calm sparked her temper. "But do you really think I'd let a few copiers and computers get in my way, Selena?"

"No." Blowing out a frustrated sigh, she added, "Look, I don't want to have this conversation in a hallway."

"Then give me the option of something more private."

"Private?"

"Yeah. Private. You and me. Nobody else."

He must have liked the kisses they'd shared as much as she had. "You don't give up, do you, Lone?" she prodded, liking the sound of his last name, how it felt in her mouth.

"No, I don't, Selena. And deep down, you don't want me to."

He was right, of course, which was why she flinched when a strong, warm hand flexed around her upper arm. She registered the contact, the warmth, the coffee-laced breath feathering her cheek. Before she could brace herself, he dragged her away from the copy machine, into a shadowy recess. "Damn," she whispered, realizing he was heading for the one place the video cameras couldn't penetrate.

"You've got a mouth on you," he said almost gruffly. "Maybe you're not as innocent as you look."

His tone gave her pause. Did he suspect something? "What do you mean?"

The low rumble of his voice shouldn't have vibrated through her, but it did. "You kiss like a woman who's thought about it a lot."

If he only knew. Her secret diary came to mind. "Well, I haven't," she lied.

"You really believe last night was a mistake?"

"Definitely."

Once more she told herself she'd only gone to Passer

la Nuit to see if he was spying on her. If he was, last night would have played out differently. He would never have talked about his passion for cracking codes, or kissed her good-night. He was working in Sensitive Data Entry for some mysterious reason, but it had nothing to do with her. "We work together," she stated again.

"That didn't bother you last night."

Anger she usually kept hidden threatened to break through to the surface, nearly surprising her with its intensity. "It's never too late for a woman to say what she wants."

"Or doesn't want."

"So back off."

Not looking the least affected by her rudeness, he drew her almost roughly against him. She should have balked, but at the commanding touch, heat tunneled through her, leaving a wide-open path for Edison. Looking into implacable eyes, she felt strangely crushed and vulnerable, and all at once she hated him for every unwanted feeling she'd experienced since their romantic dinner.

"The second you let me kiss you it was too late," Edison declared, his voice ragged, his mouth nearly on hers. "Too late when you wore that dress made for sin."

Not about to humiliate herself by wiggling away from him, she let the strong, firm hand stay on her arm, but she wished the wall wasn't behind her, that there was somewhere else to go. "We went on a date, okay? It just didn't work out."

"The way we kissed, I'd say it worked out fine."

What an understatement. She could still feel blistering heat from his soft, firm lips dragging over hers, paving the way for the slow claiming push of his tongue. Now the quick breath she drew through her teeth made them tingle. His kisses promised heavenly romance, but the hardening of his body was begging for devilish satisfaction. "I don't deny there was a physical spark."

"Was?" He chuckled softly, hoarsely. "I could have had you on your back in a heartbeat. Still could."

His conceit nearly sent her over the edge. "Some women like to be on top."

"Fine by me."

"Nobody talks to me this way."

"I do."

Her jaw slackened. "Excuse me?"

"If men haven't talked to you this way, Selena, then it's a damn shame," he retorted. He studied her for a long moment, and then, uttering a soft, explosive curse, he lifted a finger and very gently stroked it down her cheek, trailing fire. "You were hungry and wanting last night," he added, his anger over her denial of their passion laced with silk. "You were hot, vibrating with need. You were craving a man. And not just any man, Selena. Me." As if to make his point, his gaze dropped, its heat washing over where her nipples had peaked almost painfully, beading against her top. "You're still hungry, Selena."

Judging from that searing gaze, he was, too. "Hungry—" her voice suddenly caught "—for things like love and acceptance." The second the words were out, she wished she hadn't revealed so much, further exposing herself when he'd already seen more than she wanted him to.

"Love and acceptance. Who says I can't give those?"

"Get real."

"What's happening between us is as real as it gets."

He was probably right, and suddenly she wanted to be anywhere but here. She'd lived down her past, hadn't she? She'd quit being the butt of boys' jokes years ago. She'd left home for a world of danger, and when her lifestyle brought power and the license to carry a weapon, she'd finally felt in control. She'd told herself she simply didn't have time for the things most women wanted. Satisfying sex. Husbands, babies. But now she had nothing left to prove, and her life had come to a dead halt. She was supposed to confront her fears now and face the demons, so she could start chasing sexual and emotional security. Instead, a brilliant, sexy man wanted her—and she was too scared to do anything except run again.

His voice caught huskily. "It's not over, Selena."

"It?"

"We," he corrected. "We're not over."

"I believe I get a say in that."

Emotion further darkened his eyes, making the hard blue irises soften to liquid. "Why deny this?" he asked simply, suddenly looking a little lost, as if he couldn't quite figure out why Selena Silverwood should matter so much to him. "Why deny us?"

"Why?" Because she didn't dare risk trusting him. And because his kisses, like his house, had stolen her heart last night. The tiny, enchanting cottage was invisible from the street, dwarfed by trees. It had round rooms, turrets, and was made of oddly shaped patches of brick that gave way to rough-hewn stone. Inside, hardwood floors were laid with Oriental rugs, and floor-to-ceiling bookcases were messily crammed with heavy, gilt-edged books he was brilliant enough to actually read. There was even a dog to love.

And good security, Selena reminded herself. Despite its welcoming appearance, everything was protected by high-tech locks. No matter how open Edison seemed, he was as cagey as she. Besides, he never stayed with women. Really, if she wasn't so afraid of getting hurt, he'd be the perfect man to help get her sex life off the ground. Tempting, she thought, but then said, "It's just not a good time for me to get involved."

He reached again to trail that intimate finger down her cheek, then simply said, "All right." And then he shrugged, turned on his heel and headed back toward their work station.

Her lips parting in surprise, she stared at his retreating back. His leaving this way shouldn't have bothered her—they'd only gone on one date—but with each distancing step, she felt as if her heart was being ripped out of her chest. She'd secretly wanted him to stay and fight; she'd expected him to. How he'd kissed her last night had shaken her to the core. He'd felt the same, she could tell.

Which meant he was right. It wasn't over. It wouldn't be until they shared a bed. Whatever was between them seemed predestined. Fated. It was a river running its course, and she had no idea how to stop it.

But she had a job to do, dammit. A job that didn't include a sexual tryst with Edison Lone. *He'll be easy to ignore,* she tried to tell herself. *He's just a man.*

"C'MON," EDISON MUTTERED as he finished disabling Selena's keypad alarm system. Drawing a leather sheath from the inside pocket of a sports coat he wore over jeans, he removed a slender steel pick and deftly wiggled it into a lock, noting that, for a supposed data-entry assistant, Selena had top-dollar security. Not that he couldn't crack lock systems as dexterously as codes. And not that he still believed Selena Silverwood was her name.

Before 1992 she'd never even existed. It had taken a few days, but for a hefty price and a promised case of the dark home brew ale Edison made as a hobby, he'd found a hacker who could dig up the truth. Someone had put together a false identity for her, with records dating back to '92, but how had Eleanor, IBI and the CIIC missed that? Apparently, they hadn't really been looking. It was suspicious as hell. But now it was anybody's guess as to who the woman really was—and why she was at IBI. Possibly, she had friends in high places who'd fudged things so she could pass a security clearance.

"Ten more minutes," he whispered, "and maybe

we'll know what she's up to." Repocketing the picks, he glanced down the empty hallway, then gave the front door a gentle shove. Kicking off his loafers in case he was trailing mud, he closed the door, carefully explored the living room and kitchen, and then headed for her bedroom, barely able to suppress his growing anger.

He'd been had. And he didn't like being trumped by a woman he wanted in his bed. Growing up in various foster homes and boarding schools, he'd learned early on that trusting people was usually a mistake. But deep down, he'd secretly started trusting Selena. He couldn't explain why. *Call it honor among thieves,* he decided, feeling disgusted with himself as he stared into the room where she slept.

Like the rest of the place, it was too clean and empty. She definitely anticipated leaving in a hurry. Pictures lined the walls, but they were only for show, mostly prints from museums, nothing with enough personality to provide clues as to what Selena was really like.

Most closets were completely empty. The bedrooms held clothes, but no sweaters or coats, only the spring dresses she'd been wearing to IBI. Clumped together, they looked almost like uniforms, and after a moment, he realized they were hanging in the exact order in which she'd been wearing them.

Except for the silver dress. It hung apart, on a velvet hanger, and before Edison could take his eyes from it, his hand had paused, tracing crepe tatters as soft as her skin. Impulsively, he brought the fabric to his face, inhaling. "Sex," he muttered. Faint, delicate and alluring, the scent was far more interesting than what he otherwise recognized as Joy perfume. Shutting his eyes, he was gone for a second, naked and hard, lost inside Selena, or whoever she was, and now the mind-blowing scent was trailing from her slender neck...her autumnal hair...from between long legs he desperately wanted to see part for him.

"Fantasy," he muttered. "Pure damn fantasy."

He'd never allow himself to make love with her now. She was a traitor, nothing more. Just a job. A woman Eleanor and the CIIC had paid him good money to bust. As soon as he'd done his duty, he'd happily return to researching and analyzing those classified ads.

But it was a lie. Somehow, this unlikely woman had stolen his common sense. He was haunted by her awkward gangliness, enchanted by her shy smiles, astonished by the way she'd morphed from an ugly duckling into a sex siren draped in silver.

Dropping the fabric, he turned, his eyes settling on a neatly made bed, and he felt a rush of pleasure at invading her space. Call it tit for tat. Like a thief in the night, she'd stolen into his fantasies. And wasn't that more criminal than breaking into her apartment? Didn't a man have a right to the integrity of his own mind?

At least Edison wasn't suffering through office drudgery with her today. But did she miss him? Was she worried? Quite possibly, she knew who he was. Most of his undercover work involved overseas travel, studying texts that higher-ups believed were written in code, so his being assigned in Washington was unusual.

Still, given Selena's fake ID, it was hard to say who she was, or what she knew about IBI. Did she know he wasn't a temp?

He just hoped she'd believed him when he'd called in sick. Searching under the bed for her diary, he now half hoped she was onto him. In fact, he hoped she'd read his dossier and was sweating bullets.

He frowned. Where was *Night Pleasures?* Unless he cracked the code—if it *was* in code—he'd never get away from her. And he couldn't face one more day of staring at her through Plexiglas while she avoided him. "Yeah," he muttered, grunting softly as he rose from the floor. "This case has been a real day at the beach."

He slid open a bureau drawer. "Her glasses." Ever since their dinner at Passer la Nuit, she'd left them home, in favor of contacts—or at least that's what he'd thought. Now, peering through the black-framed glasses, he cursed softly. Why hadn't he guessed they were fakes? Opening the next drawer, he saw it contained dust, a few gold safety pins and a rose sachet. When he pulled out a third, he whispered, "Very nice, *mademoiselle.*"

Riotously colorful silks lay bunched together in a tumble of strings and lace, answering any questions about what Selena wore under her unrevealing dresses. Sucking in a breath, Edison hooked a finger around a black strap, lifting it until he was staring at the deep lace cups. Fishing around, he found matching panties, then a silver chain similar to the one *mademoiselle* wrapped around her waist in *Night Pleasures*.

"And speaking of *mademoiselle,*" Edison added, finding the diary. He took it out—it was pink with a border of gold scrolling—and then headed for the bed. Bunching pillows behind him, he got comfortable—not that he expected surprises, since he'd already read everything in typewritten format.

Frowning, he suddenly glanced up. Was that the door? No. He shook his head. Just his imagination. His eyes returned to the page, catching the words *She wanted him in the worst way,* and he whispered, "I'm beginning to wish she *would* come home for lunch." *Or something else.* Her bedding held the scent he'd come to recognize as distinctly hers, and it reminded him of how she'd felt in his arms—so much better than any fantasy. He opened the diary.

Tonight, the marquis had laid out what she was to wear—a crimson silk robe, complete with a thick sash—and now she was naked beneath it, the luxurious fabric gliding on her bare skin, decadent and sumptuous, making her yearn to feel the equally silken touch of her lover inside her.

He'd better come soon because she was getting drowsy. The fragrances in this room of the pleasure palace had drugged her, clouding everything but sensuous thoughts. She'd taken the jeweled pins from her hair, so the wild, honeyed strands tumbled to her waist, and now she lifted a lock and twirled it around a finger as she lazily reclined. The sleek black horsehair sofa prickled her calves, not unpleasantly, as she gazed into the aromatic smoke that swirled upward from wall-mounted censors. Dim lamps set in the stone walls glowed and the air was moist, foggy as if it were a cool summer night.

Suddenly an unseen hand seemed to press upon her chest, and she struggled up, gasping for just one breath of untainted air. But it was useless. Thousands of intoxicating scents seemed to mingle in her nostrils, then overpower her lungs: animal musk, flowers exuding pollen, hundred-year-old wine. Feeling suddenly woozy, almost faint, she used her elbows to push herself from the sofa, only to sink again, this time deeper into velvet pillows; then deeper still, until their corded gold tassels stroked her cheeks like palm fronds.

"Sleep."

"Marquis?" she whispered groggily. His voice seemed to be fluttering in her blood.

"Sleep, my darling."

"Not before we make love," she whispered back, her weak voice barely audible in the thick, drugged air.

"Lovemaking. Is that what you want?"

"Yes...oh, yes."

She turned to face him, rolling on a sea of horsehair and velvet and silk, her desire-glazed eyes seeking his. "Marquis?"

But the air was too dark and thick, his face obscured. He'd come to her naked, though, and her heart missed a beat as he crouched above her, loosening and shaking a mane of black, luxuriant hair, his movements intent with purpose. His chest was coated with course hair that narrowed to a tapering line, pulling her gaze lower, until she realized, with a sharp intake of breath, that he was dangerously aroused. Her head swam at the vision, at how the skin was darker there, at how huge he was, nestled in thick curls.

Broad hands glided over her robe, pushing it upward on her thighs, exposing flesh. A flick of his wrist dispensed with the thick sash at her waist and he parted the silk, bringing heat to her cheeks when she realized what this infernal house of pleasure had done to her.

"You want me," he murmured, sounding pleased, his searing gaze burning on her rosy, flushed skin, settling where the tips of her breasts were reddened and taut.

Leaning closer, he kissed them until she cried out, saying, "You've drugged the very air, sir."

"I'll drug your soul," he assured her. Catching her hands, he thrust them above her head, then slowly circled an aroused nipple with his tongue. Wet fire raced down her belly. Twisting with the climbing need, she glanced down, glimpsing eyes that twinkled devilishly as he molded hot, dry palms over her knees to ease them apart. "I'm going to taste you," he promised, panting raggedly, and then, when her eyes widened, he added,

"Surely you know men can pleasure women this way."

But she hadn't known. And as his mouth descended, she gasped, senselessly, instinctively trying to move away, unsure of what was happening. But it was too late. His tongue was already parting her, baring the pearl, flickering....

Groaning, Edison reeled back to the present, forgetting why he was here long enough to silently curse Selena Silverwood for her rejection. She wanted him. And he wanted her. She had a helluva lot more than sex on the brain, too. Her writing was sensual and laden with detail, which showed she dreamed of deep, lasting passion. But she was avoiding him.

Blowing out an annoyed sigh, he ignored his arousal and reread the entry, studying the handwriting.

It was definitely suspicious. Upper flourishes of letters bled into the lines above, a known indicator of unsatisfied sexual impulses. "I understand the feeling," he muttered. Shifting uncomfortably, he tried not to react to the obvious excitement she'd been feeling as she wrote, but her words ran together. Letters sprawled wildly. Text ran into the side margins, crowding the pages, as if there wasn't room enough for her explosive need. There was no bottom margin at all, which meant that, in addition to being a dreamer and a loner, she was capable of traveling into her own subconscious.

Which was where the marquis resided. He was elusive, his face always hidden, and Edison couldn't help but wonder who had served as her inspiration for the man. "The pen pressure's deceptive, too," he murmured. Some letters weren't joined, indicating she lacked a normal sense of connectedness. Even worse, she slanted her letters to the left, which showed she had a taste for deception.

He just wished he wasn't fighting a little voice that said maybe she was a mixed-up neophyte who'd fallen in with the wrong crowd and gotten herself into a jam. Maybe somebody was blackmailing her into stealing from IBI. Either way, if her diary was written in code here, it looked nearly impossible to crack.

Drawing a pen and notebook from his jacket pocket, Edison placed them on the bed, so he could take notes while he read, and began working again.

> "Give yourself to the pleasure," the marquis coached, the gentle assault of his mouth so masterful that it pulled soft cries from her throat....

It was almost five o'clock when Edison forced himself to replace the diary. She'd be home from IBI any minute, and he had to get out of here, but it was tempting to stay. Lying in bed, reading her fantasies, he'd felt every bit as passionate as the marquis. Trouble was, Selena was lying. In addition to the information he'd gotten from the hacker, analyzing her handwriting had completely reversed any ideas he'd had about her innocence.

He still wanted her, though. On his way out, he

opened the closet again, just to glimpse the silver dress. Feeling instantly hard at the recollection of how she'd looked wearing it, he groaned. On impulse, he lithely swooped down and hooked a finger beneath the heel of a matching silver shoe, a slow smile curling his lips.

Given how she'd played Cinderella, shouldn't he take a memento? Wasn't that exactly what she deserved? Shouldn't she share the frustration he was feeling? His smile broadened as he dropped the shoe, toe down, into his jacket pocket.

When he slipped out the door moments later, reactivating the keypad alarm, he was actually grinning, imagining the stunned look on her face when she realized her come-hither pump was gone.

4

SOMETHING IN HER BEDROOM was out of place. Selena was sure of it, but she pushed aside the thought, concentrating on her phone conversation with her editor, Kate Bernstein. "You're not interrupting my writing Kate. I've just got a lot on my mind tonight."

"You should! You're about to become a household name."

"Oh, please!" Shaking Edison from her thoughts, as well as her upcoming meeting with the person for whom she was working, Selena laughed for the first time today, not about to let the compliments go to her head. "Look, everything's fine. I'm moving right along with the diary." Wedging the cordless phone between her cheek and shoulder, she leaned back at the desk, studying the open book. "I'm reworking the one about the swimming pool, but I'm hoping we can keep the fantasy about the wall of mirrors just as it is. The scene on the horsehair sofa, too."

"One of my favorites," Kate agreed, her voice crackling with New York energy. "Your diary's going to be big," she added enthusiastically. "You'll push Nancy Friday off the map."

"Now, now," Selena chided with another chuckle. "I think the world's big enough for both of us."

"Not according to your mother."

"She's definitely my biggest supporter," conceded Selena. Her mother had unearthed the diary in the trailer Selena kept parked on the family farm, and waving away her daughter's mortification, she'd said Selena possessed a true gift, a voice to which other women would respond. Without telling her, she'd sent the book to an agent, who had, in turn, found Kate.

"Women need to open up," Kate was saying now. "We've come a long way, baby, but we've still got a ways to go."

Despite her worries, Selena grinned. "My mother's sentiments, exactly."

"What do you expect?" Kate laughed appreciately. "Your mother was a sixties' protester, right? Didn't she even get arrested during the war?"

"More than once," Selena said dryly. "She met my father in a lockup during the Chicago riots."

"Your father must really be something, to fall for such a strong, self-starting woman."

"He is." Selena's heart warmed, gave a tug as she thought of home. As impossible as her adjustment to country living during her high school years had been, she loved her parents and the life they'd made for themselves.

"It's so great," Kate sighed wistfully, "to have a mom who was a champion for women's rights and free love."

"Free love?" Selena could only shake her head.

"She's been happily and monogamously married to my father for thirty-five years."

Kate's voice was arch. "Are you implying your mother's liberalism is merely lip service?"

"Yeah. But don't spread it around. The information would crush her." Her eyes panning the nearly bare bedroom, Selena felt her heart tug again at thoughts of her tumbledown trailer nestled in the woods at her folks' farm, and of her other Washington apartment. Teeming with personality, both places put this beige bedroom to shame, and she couldn't help but wonder if Edison would be impressed. Not that he'd ever see them, she reminded herself. Her thoughts drifted to him as Kate continued chattering over sounds of sirens and honking horns.

Suddenly, Selena frowned and straightened in the chair. Yes...there it was again. Her sixth sense had kicked in, warning her. But what was the source of the red flag? Something in the room was definitely out of place. Squinting, she took in the neatly made bed, then the open closet door. When had the uneasy feeling first hit her?

After I got undressed.

Coming in from IBI, she'd kicked off her shoes in the closet and traded her dress for a soft terry robe. Just as she'd turned away, her hand had stilled on the knob and, for a second, she'd had the sudden, distinct impression that Edison Lone was in the room. He wasn't, of course, and since their tête-a-tête near the copy machine, she'd kept to her side of the Plexiglas. So why was she smelling his hard-to-define scent in her bedroom?

Pure fantasy, she thought. She wanted him, and wishful thinking was making her mind play tricks. In reality, she'd asked him to back off. And he had. She should count herself lucky. Probing the secured files at IBI was no easy task with the firm's best cryptanalyst seated within spitting distance. But what if she'd been wrong to discourage him? After all, she'd wanted to seduce him, hadn't she? Besides, if somebody ratted her out at IBI, maybe he'd cut her some slack. Obscure what she was really up to from Eleanor Luders and her superiors.

She started. "Hmm? What was that, Kate?"

"Haven't you been listening?"

"Trying," Selena confessed. "As I said, I've got too much on my mind right now."

"Well, make your wildest fantasies your top priority," encouraged Kate. "Our editor-in-chief is sure your diary will be the next bestseller, so she's bumping up its publication in the schedule."

Selena tried not to panic. "Bumping it up?"

"We're going into hardcover first, not paperback. And in December, not June. It's going to be marketed as a Christmas book, so you've got to get to work."

She chewed her lip nervously. It was Friday now, and on Sunday she had to meet her contact on the Capitol lawn. She had precious little to give him, and Dean Meade wasn't particularly nice when displeased.

"Can you pull the diary entries together in another week?"

Another week? "Sure."

"I don't want to edit until it's exactly as you want it."

Somehow, she'd do it. If her diary really did become a bestseller, she could kiss Dean Meade—and everybody else she'd ever had to work for—goodbye. She could retire. *And start a family. Isn't that what you want? Great sex with a guy who loves you—and a bundle of joy?* The voice sounded from somewhere so deep within her that it was easy enough to push away.

"And you want to publish under a pseudonym?" Kate asked.

Selena came back to the present. "Just the name Silence."

"Love it," enthused Kate. "Marketing can do a lot with that. We like the whole idea of women who've been silent about their fantasies finally being able to speak out."

Selena shrugged. "It works for me. My parents almost named me Silence." She suddenly laughed. "My grandmothers had conniption fits, so everybody settled on a more conservative first name. Anyway, I want a pseudonym. I'd feel uncomfortable meeting strangers who knew what was going on in the deepest reaches of my imagination."

"Fair enough," Kate pronounced. "Well, I should go. I met a guy from Wall Street who's taking me out for drinks. How about you? I didn't figure I'd catch a woman with your imaginative skills at home alone on Friday night."

She thought of Edison. Surely his reasons for being in

Sensitive Data Entry had nothing to do with her, and now he'd called in sick. She imagined him curled sulkily on a sofa, half-dressed, flipping through channels with a remote control device. "I *would* go out," Selena deadpanned. "But a New York editor's chained me to a desk. Deadlines, you know how it goes."

"Sure do," replied Kate. "I've discovered that people will work you to death anytime you let them. That's why I religiously blow off the deadlines and go out."

"Granting me permission to do that?"

"Take a break," counseled Kate. "It'll give you a fresh start tomorrow."

Kate had no inkling of the pressures haunting Selena. Still, maybe it wouldn't hurt to take Edison some chicken soup. Just because she'd asked him to back off sexually didn't mean they couldn't be friends, did it? As the days wore on, she'd found herself wanting a truce. And wasn't it her place to ask for it? Sure, he was a nuisance while she was secretly trying to get information at IBI, but one of these days he might be a good friend to have.

Saying her goodbyes, Selena set the cordless phone aside and gazed down at her open diary, which she'd been revising. "The drugged air was dark and thick," she read, "his face obscured. He'd come to her naked, and her heart missed a beat as she saw him hovering above her, his raven mane falling over liquid eyes that were just as dark with purpose."

Sighing, Selena imagined the rest: tangled chest hair curling between her fingers; hard, rippling ridges of ribs; her hands falling to where he was aroused. Lost in fantasy, she sought the man's eyes—and realized she wasn't looking at the marquis. She was staring at Edison Lone.

"What would it hurt to see him?" she murmured, knowing it was useless to fight such strong impulses. "And what would I wear?"

Wishing she had jeans and T-shirts, she frowned, headed for the closet and lifted out a skirt that was ankle length. Made of black-white-and-tan animal-print fabric, it had a side slit. If she wore it with the white leotard tank top she used for workouts, she wouldn't look as if she'd just stepped from an office.

Pulling the skirt from a hanger, she suddenly paused, tilting her head. There it was again. That odd, unsettling feeling that Edison had been in her bedroom. Intently, she scrutinized her clothes, but nothing seemed amiss. "You're getting paranoid," she said. It wasn't the first time, and she did have her reasons.

"But it's strange," she muttered. She shook her head, dispensing with Edison's phantom presence. And then she began to dress.

"EVENTUALLY YOU'RE GOING to have to help me catch M," Edison said with a casualness he didn't really feel. Shooing away a mosquito he leaned farther back in one of the wrought-iron chaise longues on the stone patio, still processing the fact that Selena Silverwood, or whoever she was, had shown up on his doorstep tonight.

"Eventually," she replied flippantly. "Good word."

In the darkness, his eyes trailed over her outfit. Her skirt was wet at midthigh from where M had leaped from his bath to greet her. "And if I'm lucky," she added dryly, lifting a long-necked bottle of Edison's home brew from the round table between them, "eventually won't come. So far, nabbing your dog's been about as easy as—"

"He's not my dog."

She chuckled. "Still holding out hope for adoption?"

"Hey, what about you?" he retorted. "Want to be a parent? It could happen tonight."

She clearly caught his double meaning, the arch of her brow assuring him they wouldn't be heading for a bedroom anytime soon. "You really think I'm that easy a mark?"

Edison shrugged, telling himself he wasn't about to sleep with a traitor, anyway. "It was worth a shot. Wouldn't you like something warm to cuddle up with on those long winter nights?"

"It's not even summer yet."

"Yeah, but winter comes quickly."

"I'll think about it," she promised, the soft teasing light in her eyes saying she understood he was offering himself as the something warm. "But trying to take that dog to my place would be like wrestling a greased watermelon."

"Some metaphor," he murmured, wondering where she was from. Was she a city girl? Country girl? Nothing in her apartment had given him a hint. "Wrestled many greased watermelons?"

"Do you always notice metaphors?"

"Sure," he said, keeping his tone casual. "I'm a teacher."

When she turned to face him, her eyes were the gold of autumn twilight. "I've wrestled a few in my time."

"You make it sound tough."

"Like alligators."

He couldn't help but bait her. "You live dangerously?"

Feeling disturbed that she only took the jibe as flirtation, he vaguely wondered if she was so criminal she couldn't even feel guilt.

"I don't live any more dangerously than you," she answered.

What was that supposed to mean? Did she know he was really a code cracker? He was half tempted to ask, but direct questions were always so unprofessional. Besides, he was enjoying their game. He arched an eyebrow. "I look dangerous, huh?"

She tilted her head, considering, and suddenly the night air seemed pregnant with the secrets between them. After a moment, she smiled. "Not when you let a four-pound Maltese get the best of you."

Edison frowned. "Is that what he is?"

"Half Maltese, half poodle. That would be my guess."

"Don't tell me. You breed dogs as a hobby?"

"Only in my checkered youth."

"A checkered youth," he echoed.

At that, she fell silent, as if there might be some truth

to it, and Edison's gaze followed hers as she stared across the lush backyard, past a gas grill and a full, sudsy keg tub where he'd been washing M, toward a stone walkway that curled around to the front of the cottage. The evening had been unseasonably hot, as if summer were testing things, putting a toe into the water, deciding whether or not to make its appearance this year, but as the darkness deepened, the air had chilled. Her eyes traced the top of the privacy fence that circled the yard.

"It's getting cooler," she finally said.

"Yeah." Since he'd been washing the dog, he was clad only in khaki shorts, and he was starting to wish for shoes and a shirt. Not that he much wanted to move when Selena's eyes kept lingering on his chest, and when the twilight was so right, and when the fireflies were still swarming in the black, silhouetted bushes. Dimly, he could hear far-off traffic, but sounds of nature were louder: frogs that had managed to survive in the heart of D.C., the high whine of crickets. His eyes took in where blades of shadow cast by some basketed ferns jagged across Selena's pale face, throwing stripes against the black, woven pattern of her chaise.

Nearly lost in the shadows, she seemed to be dressed in camouflage. Or as if she were a wild jungle creature who'd sought refuge in his yard. And maybe she was. He could swear she was scanning the ten-foot privacy fence again, taking in the gate and the upper perimeter, which was wired with electronic sensors. Absently taking another sip of ale, he wondered how aware she was of the state-of-the-art security. Hell, maybe she was jealous. His was even better than what she'd installed at her apartment, and that was saying something.

She squinted. "Where did he go, anyway?"

Edison gestured with the tilted neck of the bottle, thinking she was even more elusive than the dog and wondering once more why she'd come. "He's under that rhododendron."

"Ah." Abruptly, she laughed, the low, throaty sound curling into his blood as she watched M rooting beneath a bush, kicking up sprays of brown dirt that clung to his wet white hair.

Another slow sip of ale slid coolly down his throat, then Edison sighed. "When you got here, he was almost clean, you know."

"So was I."

Her voice sent another thrill through him, one he knew he couldn't ignore much longer, not when he'd spent the afternoon in her bed, playing hooky from IBI and reading her diary. Wishing she hadn't just called attention to the disheveled state of her outfit, he let his eyes drift down her reclining body. How had he thought her awkward? Lying on the chaise, she looked sleek and feline wrapped in animal prints, her bare arms elegant, the slit in her skirt open to the thigh, exposing plenty of smooth leg. "Sure hope you didn't take a bath on my account," he murmured. "I'd just hate to think I put you out."

She grinned, her teeth flashing white in the dim light.

"Don't flatter yourself. And anyway, would you really have preferred me to visit you dirty?"

She hadn't meant any innuendo, but suddenly he was thinking of a million things he could do with her that a prude would definitely term dirty. His voice dropped, becoming almost lost to the night. "I'll take you any way you come." While she registered the comment, he realized it was true. As soon as she'd gotten here, she'd filled his house, her scent permeating the air. Too much, he'd liked the compliments she'd lavished on his little slice of heaven in the city as she'd first surveyed it. "Chicken soup?" he'd asked, staring at her.

She'd held up two containers. "And ice cream."

He'd felt as if he'd been caught red-handed, since a long-necked ale bottle dangled from his hand. "Thanks."

She'd looked embarrassed. "I thought you were sick. Guess you were just taking a personal day?"

He'd convinced her that he'd recovered, and then decided she'd come for a truce. But why? He was beyond flattering himself into thinking she wanted to scratch a female itch. That would be too much to hope for. Besides, she was too complicated to be ruled by such simple urges. She'd seemed sincere, too, commenting on his house, his books, his yard, and she'd laughed, enjoying his stories about how M was failing the obedience school he'd started this week.

Now Edison felt edgy again and blamed her for his discomfort. If he needed a woman, he took her straight to bed. The method was plain and simple and uncomplicated and, so far, it had always worked. "C'mon," he said gruffly, setting aside his ale. "What say we grab M and get him cleaned up?"

She was already gliding sinuously from the chaise into the yard, the dew-damp grass darkening the fabric of her flats. "Is this how you torture all your visitors?" she called over her shoulder. "Making them get soaked to the bone on your behalf?"

"The behalf of my dog," he corrected.

"I thought it *wasn't* your dog. Careful," she warned. "Or it's you who'll have company on those long winter nights."

"Company's fine," he informed her. "Just not dogs."

"M," she called playfully. "Come here, you little rat."

"Aren't you the cat's meow," Edison muttered, his lips parting in surprise as M jumped to attention at the sound of her voice. The little dog cocked his head and peered out from beneath the leaves of the rhododendron, surveying Selena as she crouched.

"Come here, you miserable little troublemaker."

Edison had to give her credit. If the standard rules about puppies and babies applied, the woman calling herself Selena Silverwood was trustworthy. With a quick, gleeful yap, M raced toward her. Jumping a clear foot off the ground, he lunged, wiggling, into her arms, and she moaned with humor as dirt streaked across her previously white tank top.

Edison winced. "Sorry about your shirt."

"No problem."

Chuckling softly, he decided he liked that about her.

He'd dated plenty of women who wouldn't so much as polish sterling silver without gloves. "That's the first time I've ever seen him come on command. Maybe I should be paying you, not an obedience school."

"Maybe," she agreed dryly. "From what you said about the expense of the school, it'd be more economical to put M through Harvard."

Watching her, thinking of college educations, he wondered if she'd ever considered taking on the responsibility of kids, but he didn't dwell on the thought. "Here," he murmured, striding toward the tub. "I'd better help."

"We're fine." Sinking to her knees in the grass, she slowly lowered M to the tub. But that was where the seamless choreography ended. Right before M's feet hit the now-cold suds, sharp yaps pierced the air. Suspended above the water, the dirt-covered dog looked like a hamster on a wheel, his legs pumping madly. When his paws hit, suds spewed. He twisted his tiny body—right, then left—writhing as the terrified, ear-splitting yaps gave way to a menacing back-of-the-throat growl. Baring his teeth, he gave a final jerk, springing from Selena's grasp and splashing into the tub.

"He'll drown!" she gasped, both her hands plunging under the suds for the dog.

"Arff!"

A wave of water arced into her face. Two paws shot from the suds and hooked on the rim of the tub, then M surfaced, looking like a drowned rat. Attempting to grasp his middle, Selena careened sideways. Sensing what was about to happen, Edison clutched at her, managing to catch the strappy shoulder of her tank top. The move brought him, quite literally, to his own knees, and he gasped as his groin connected with her hip. When she grabbed the tub for balance, it tipped.

The physical contact, coupled with the frigid wave of water that soaked his shorts, made him reflexively tighten his fingers around her shoulder strap. And then he heard it rip. Softly cursing, he half rose, righting the empty tub. M was long gone, streaking for the bushes as Edison disengaged his fingers from the mangled strap. He hauled Selena swiftly upward. She bounced against his chest, and he instinctively drew her close.

They sprung apart then, wide-eyed, like teenagers caught in the act. But they weren't teenagers. They were aroused adults who'd been teasing each other for days. Both were drenched, clothes clinging, and he was staring where her dirty wet shirt was plastered to her chest, the tattered strap flapping at the shoulder. His heart was hammering, the back of his throat dry now, as if filled with sawdust. "You're wet," he managed to state.

"Yeah. Can't argue with you there."

His hand tightened around her upper arm, and eyes he couldn't control studied her breasts through the nearly transparent leotard and flimsy bra. Taking in the fleshy mounds, which were tinged with blessedly dark color, he felt his groin tug, his own drenched shorts pulling. Her breasts looked painfully, achingly ready for the salve of his mouth.

Despite the darkness of the patio, he could see high color rising in her cheeks, how the excited pulse at her throat flickered. Her breath caught. "Eventually," he murmured.

"Eventually," she said as she had before, when he said they'd have to catch M. "Good word."

"Isn't it?" he replied, enjoying how alive her skin felt beneath his touch. Frustrated need surged, flooding him with heat as his gaze raked down her body, as viscerally as a touch. Leaning nearer and nuzzling her neck with the stubble of his chin, he lavished a never-ending kiss down the slender column, murmuring, "Eventually's not for a long time, Selena."

"No?" she whispered, arching instinctively, pressing her soft mound very close to where he'd become so hard for her. *Close,* he thought in a rush of desire. But not *there.* His eyes had locked on the mouth he meant to kiss.

"You can't leave before you get what you came for."

"Presumptuous," she whispered back, "aren't you?"

"No," he countered. "But I know what you need."

"Then give it to me."

Her unexpected boldness was like a fire. It lit beneath him, around him, inside him. "I don't make a woman ask twice," he assured her softly, quickly bringing his lips to hers and letting passion guide him. He sighed. She sighed. And then there was only the slow sliding velvet of melding tongues, a clicking of teeth, the mindless exploration of soft inner cheeks. Rubbing a thumb into the hollow of her shoulder, he caressed under the strap, where her shirt hung by a thread, and then the thumb dipped under the neckline.

"Arch for me, Selena," he urged, palming a breast, while putting pressure on the small of her back. "Arch." His mouth was wet against hers as he fingered the water-dampened ridges of her spine. Shuddering, he suddenly realized he couldn't take it. He was too unbearably aroused. This woman could send him over the edge. He drew back anyway, realigning their hips so she could better feel the age-old, insufferable heat that was driving him.

"Edison," she said breathlessly.

But that was all he let her say. His mouth was on hers again, locked so tightly that no words could be spoken. The kiss was pure sex; what it did to their bodies, merciless. Her head was angled back in rapture, and he was hungrily pushing up her shirt and unhooking the front clasp of her bra. Slowing, he worked each nipple, teasing them until he fed one to his waiting lips. Groaning at her taste and struggling against the power of his response, he suckled hard, his tongue flickering....

Images from her diary flooded his mind, and he fantasized he was the marquis. In reality, he was gliding a hand down her cold, wet skirt. He found the slit, a strip of bare thigh, and pushed upward until his fingers found soaked panties. Gasping, he explored where the tub's cold water gave way to something hot.

But she suddenly tensed, and only then did Edison realize how far gone he was. Later, he wasn't sure why he made the next move. Maybe he wanted to punish her. In the heat of the moment, he knew he'd probably steal IBI secrets *for* her, if she asked him to, and he hated the fact that he was this out of control.

"I didn't mean to flinch," she whispered, knowing exactly what he was reacting to. The admission seemed to cost her. "I...I don't want you to stop, Edison. But I got nervous...."

She should be. After all, she was probably stealing from IBI. Cursing under his breath, he tried not to notice how gorgeous she looked, with her wet shirt pushed above her breasts, her bra open and hazy shadows playing on her flesh. Her flushed face was veiled by darkness.

The words seemed to come from outside himself. "You don't really want me, do you, Selena?"

Her voice was husky. "I do."

"But you tensed. The body doesn't lie, does it?"

With those words, he simply turned and headed for the back door, leaving her on the patio. He was aware she was still behind him. He was aware he was acting like a real bastard. He heard a sudden wet slap of fabric—presumably she'd hooked her bra and was yanking down her shirt.

"I'll see myself out," she snapped furiously at his back before he closed the door.

SELENA HAD LEFT by the side entrance, her wet flats dripping on a winding stone walkway she'd previously thought charming. She'd driven straight home, and now was pacing around her bedroom. "What just happened?" she asked herself in shock.

She hadn't gone to Edison Lone's for anything remotely sexual. She'd gone to take him ice cream and chicken soup. "Like any adult would," she muttered, raking her fingers through hair he'd left incurably tangled.

"I just don't get it," she whispered, remembering the strength in his body as he'd held her, and how aroused he'd felt. He'd wanted her. She was sure of it. Her belly fluttered, then something warm and unwanted curled up inside her, making her heart pull.

"Maybe you're being too hard on him," she whispered. She'd read his file. Abandoned by parents he claimed not to remember and whom he'd never bothered to find, he was as disinclined to make attachments as she, but for different reasons. No, he'd never been physically attacked as she'd been, but he was running from love. Her eyes suddenly stung. It seemed so sad. Here they were, two full-grown, sexually attracted people who weren't even so much as satisfying a mutual itch.

Not that she'd go back to IBI now. To hell with this job. She wasn't facing Edison Lone again. Heading to the closet for a robe, she began stripping off the wet clothes. As her bra and panties hit the floor, she found herself staring at the dress she'd worn to Passer la Nuit. As she kicked off her wet flats, she glanced downward, and hairs suddenly prickled at her nape. "Where's my shoe?" Why was only one of her silver pumps on the floor of the closet?

Whipping her head around, she stared toward the bureau, trying to deny her own suspicions. On impulse, she strode to the underwear drawer and pulled out the diary. Earlier this evening, had she found it where she'd left it? Hadn't it been nestled farther down, under her black panties?

Hands trembling, she weaved toward the bed, sank onto the mattress and slowly began turning the pages, wondering what she expected to find. "Shoes don't walk away," she murmured, her eyes darting to the closet. Suddenly, she grabbed the pillow behind her, lifted it and pressed it to her face.

Edison.

She could smell him. "I'm going crazy," she muttered, assuring herself she'd only misplaced the shoe. *But that's impossible! Where?*

She was still wondering when her finger traced down the words, *Broad hands glided over her robe, pushing it upward on her thighs, exposing flesh. A flick of his wrist dispensed with the thick sash at her waist, and he parted the silk, bringing heat to her cheeks when she realized what this infernal house of pleasure had done to her.*

Selena's finger stilled on the page. She swallowed hard, vaguely aware that her throat was tightening. There, visible on the paper and feeling like silk on her fingertip, was a black hair, one so soft and dark that it had to be Edison Lone's.

5

"SO MUCH FOR YOUR PLAN to distract Edison Lone." His lover's husky voice was hushed, her red-lipsticked mouth curling with displeasure as she casually seated herself behind him on the steps of the Lincoln Memorial. In the next few days, they'd be selling the mother lode, a catalog of U.S. arsenal supplies, to a hungry little third world country.

After that, they'd be home free. Thumbing through the pages of one of the city's free newspapers, he opened it to the classifieds, reviewing an ad he'd placed under a false name. "Introducing Edison Lone and Selena Silverwood was a plan you approved of a few days ago," he reminded her.

"You said she was only an assistant," she snarled.

Hidden behind the newspaper, he made the mistake of looking over his shoulder. Sleek and leggy, his lover reminded him of the million-dollar mares he bet on at the track. Well bred and high-strung, the horses' perfect flanks quivered with power, their long, well-muscled legs twitching with the inborn need to race. Just like those horses, she needed careful handling. He loved her, but he was beginning to suspect she was double-crossing him, setting him up to take a fall while she left

Washington with their IBI winnings and another man, maybe her husband.

"Quit staring at me," she murmured. "Here's what you *should* be looking at." Withdrawing grainy photos from a shoulder bag, she dropped them over his shoulder, into the crease of the open tabloid. "I took these."

He shrugged. "We already know Edison and Selena are going at it hot and heavy."

"That's not even her real name. I thought your department checked her out."

"When her diary came to our attention, we did. She seemed to be an assistant, nothing more." He continued shuffling through the photos: the two of them embracing against a black compact car outside Passer la Nuit; a deep tongue kiss on a stone patio surrounded by a privacy fence.

"That's his house," she said, noting details of the security system.

"Good," he said. "And from the picture, you can see the layout. If we need to, we can break in."

"Or send someone else."

"We can't trust anybody else," he retorted. "Are you having any luck finding out her real name?"

When she shook her head, a lock of wavy hair fell over her left eye, making her look like Veronica Lake. "Nothing's verifiable. It's buried deep. Maybe she's stealing information, too."

"Like us?" He shook his head. "More likely, she works for CIIC. Maybe Lone contacted them, and he and Selena are trading information."

"No. She's been at IBI for eight months, and he didn't mention his hunch about the classified ads until last week."

"Maybe he's been researching and analyzing them longer than he let on." Impulsively, he reached behind him and trailed a finger down her calf. He'd never let anything come between him and this woman. Not her husband. Or the woman calling herself Selena Silverwood. Or Edison Lone. The closer the time came to leave the country, the edgier he got. Surely the sense that he was being double-crossed was wrong. "Don't worry, love," he murmured.

"Don't worry? What are we going to do with these two?"

"Exactly what we did last time someone was onto us."

"You mean that snitch from CIIC? Bruce Levinson?"

"Yes," he said simply. "She's probably his replacement and, as you suggested the other day, we may have to find a...more permanent solution."

"If they disappear right now, it'll look suspicious."

He nodded. "But we'll be gone. And if they're not around, no one will have access to whatever information they've found. CIIC will assume we've done something wrong, since we'll have left the country, but..."

"They won't know what. And no one will have proof."

SOMEONE WAS FOLLOWING HER. As sure as she was that Edison had read her diary and stolen her shoe, Selena was certain somebody was a hundred feet behind her. Somehow, she doubted it was a friendly somebody.

The night had turned cool and, hugging the diary and a cotton sweater to her chest, she wished she'd worn something other than one of the unassuming ankle-length skirts that Dean Meade insisted she wear to IBI. She'd have been more comfortable in the black tights she used for exercising, and less noticeable in the dark. If whoever was following her attacked, and if she needed to use her feet to kick, she might wind up tangled in her own skirt.

She pushed aside the unsettling thought. Up ahead, across the street, she saw the park where Dean wanted to meet. Why did he always choose the most isolated spots, insist on late-night meetings, and change times and places at the last minute?

"Because he's a total control freak," Selena whispered, her eyes sharpening with purpose, darting down the seemingly empty sidewalk. She was far enough from storefronts to act quickly if someone lunged from the shadows, and yet close enough to see any reflections in the window glass. Hopefully, she'd glimpse whoever was tailing her.

Somebody at IBI's onto me. And if it's the wrong person, I could wind up with my own knife in my back. Not that she couldn't react. Years ago, on a dark, dirt road in the country overhung with hardwood trees, she'd learned the importance of defending herself against men. Since then, she'd made sure she was well trained in everything from steel weapons to martial arts. *La Femme Se-*

lena, she thought, hoping to amuse herself despite the circumstances.

"Yeah, right," she whispered.

La Femme Selena hadn't even managed to adhere to rule one: never become involved with a suspect. Not that she and Edison were really involved. And after the way he'd rejected her, she'd love to find him guilty of wrongdoing, not that he was really a suspect anymore, either. Since he'd been working in Sensitive Data Entry, she'd been able to keep an eye on him, and she was convinced he was clean. Too bad. She'd like nothing more than to lock him away—at least when she wasn't having wild sensual fantasies about him.

Shaking her head in self-disgust, she felt for the knife at her waist. Barely concealed, the razor-sharp, three-inch blade was snugly sheathed in a tan leather holder that hooked over the belt to her skirt. No, she didn't need men to protect her. But she needed them for other things. Just thinking of what she and Edison had done on his patio made her knees weaken. He'd been hungry. Ravenous. His lust all-consuming.

Then he'd rejected her cold.

Shades of the past, she thought, images from a high school dance flashing through her mind, her cheeks warming with remembered mortification. Despite herself, she heard a voice she rarely allowed to surface: *why didn't Edison want me? Why can't he love me? Is there something wrong with me? And was he really in my apartment? Did he take my shoe?*

And read my diary? If so, how could he take liberties

with something so private? So special? She felt violated, and yet she couldn't help but wonder about his reaction. Deep down, she craved knowing a man with whom she could share her most private, sensual thoughts....

At least her anger was bringing everything into tighter focus. In the park up ahead, the trees looked stark, sharply delineated. A winding, paved path curled through them; banked by an overhang of branches, it led to a fenced-in playground. The path reminded her of the dark country road where she'd nearly, very unwillingly, lost her virginity. A week later, she'd left home for a fat camp, intending to lose every last ounce of extra weight. Then she'd gone to army boot camp, and the rest, including her recruitment into CIIC, was history.

Or was it? Sadness knifing into her, Selena tried not to dwell on how last night had made her think in terms not of the past, but of the future. She'd worked so hard, slimmed down, made a life for herself. Wasn't love supposed to come now? Consenting adults sharing passion? Wild, crazy sex that lasted for days?

She sighed wistfully, thinking of how passionately Edison had kissed her last night. Once more, sudsy water was soaking her breasts and chill air was teasing them, followed by Edison's soothing mouth. Feeling brazen, she'd felt the velvet night invading her mind as she'd shamelessly ground her hips against his. A bubbling cauldron of explosive need had buoyed her, making her light-headed with desire for the endlessly delicious sensations. She'd been close, right on the brink of total pleasure, when he'd abruptly turned and gone inside.

He had no idea what his rejection meant to her. It had been so hard to go to his house. Oh, she couldn't admit it yesterday, but she'd been hoping they'd have sex. Secretly, she'd imagined him ripping off her clothes, carrying her upstairs to his bed. She could still hear him whispering, "I know what you want, Selena."

And how she'd whispered back, like a fool, "Give it to me."

How humiliating! He'd left her standing there, half-undressed. If she ever saw him again, she'd tear him apart, limb from limb, just like those women in ancient Greek mythology.

"The bacchantes?" she muttered. "Or were they called Furies?" Quickly, she added, "Just ask Einstein. I mean Edison." He was no English teacher, but the books crammed in his shelves attested to his being well read. "Bacchanites," she whispered. "That's what they were called." And anyway, it didn't matter. The important thing was that they destroyed men such as Edison Lone.

Startled, she stopped abruptly. She was on the jogging path now, under the dark canopy of trees, and she needed to pay attention. A CIIC operative had wound up dead while undercover at IBI, and if Selena wasn't careful, she'd be next. She was cursing Edison for picking a fine time to invade her consciousness when a footstep sounded behind her. She spun around, registering the shadow of a gun on the blacktop. Inhaling sharply, she was sure the breath was her last.

Dean Meade stepped from the shadows, pocketing the gun. "You alone, Selena?"

Her lips parted in indignation. "You almost gave me a heart attack," she huffed. "What do you think? That I brought some lady friends along for tea?"

Ignoring her pique, Dean glanced around, looking more like a thug than the director of domestic operations at CIIC. Nearly bald, he was five inches shorter than Selena, stocky, his limbs and torso bulging with muscle that made a dark windbreaker and faded jeans look too small for him. He glanced at the diary. "What's with the book?"

"After my lady friends and I have tea," she retorted, her lips still parted in astonishment at how he'd sneaked up on her, "I thought I'd read a few inspirational passages."

Dean didn't look convinced. "An inspirational book, huh?"

The truth was, she'd been too angry to work in the apartment after realizing Edison had probably been there, so she'd taken the diary to a café. There, a kindly Italian woman who understood man trouble had nodded sympathetically and plied her with cappuccinos. As wired as she felt from the caffeine, she still wasn't going to run off at the mouth and tell Dean that her sensual fantasies were being published. He still looked curious, so she added, "The book's just something personal, okay, Dean?"

"Personal?" The disappointed tone and look of slight offense made it clear that, when it came to her life outside CIIC, he couldn't care less. "Well," he began impatiently, shifting the topic. "You're my top agent. Don't tell me you didn't find anything yet."

"My, my, you're in a good mood."

"Just cut to the chase. What did you find?"

Not nearly as much as she'd hoped. "Edison Lone's clean."

"You're sure?"

She nodded. "Yeah."

"And that's all you found out about him?"

Whatever else she'd discovered, she intended to keep it to herself. She might be publishing her sexual fantasies, but otherwise, she wasn't exactly an advocate of kiss and tell. "He's clean as a whistle."

Not looking particularly impressed by the information, Dean blew out a short, perturbed sigh. "What about the other people in his department?"

"I'm still watching Eleanor Luders."

Dean nodded toward a bench. "Want to park your butt?"

"Thanks." Seating herself, she plunged into an account of her activities at IBI while Dean sat beside her, listening. When she was done, she narrowed her eyes. Until now, she'd assumed that the presence she'd sensed was Dean's. But someone else was out there in the dark, watching them. Her eyes darted through the trees. "Dean—" despite the sudden thud of her heart, she kept her voice level "—I've got a gut feeling we really do have company."

"If all you've got's a gut feeling, then you're losing your edge. Should I put in a request to have you evaluated?"

Her lips pursed defiantly. "I'm not losing my edge."

Dean gave a bored sigh. "Well, don't turn around now, but there's a guy a hundred feet away, behind the trunk of a sycamore tree that's sandwiched between a phone pole and the gate that opens onto the kid's playground."

"You sure pick interesting moments to showcase your detection skills," she managed to reply. What was the problem with men, anyway? Hadn't Dean intended to alert her to the danger? "Since you're so observant," she couldn't help but add in a whisper, a chill slowly working its way down her spine, "you wouldn't happen to know who this person is, would you?"

"Sure." Dean sent her a long sideways glance. "It's the suspect you've been screwing on CIIC time, Selena." She was still gaping, preparing to say she wasn't having sex with anyone—and that with her bad luck, she probably never would—when Dean added, "It's Edison Lone."

As if she hadn't guessed.

HIGH-PITCHED YAPS assaulted Edison as he came inside the darkened house. "It's only me," he muttered, "but if anybody breaks in, maybe I'll get lucky and they'll take you." Unaffected by the comments, M trotted behind him, wagging his tail as Edison opened the refrigerator, stared inside and took out a bottle of home brew. After a second's deliberation, he changed his mind, grabbed the Wild Turkey and a shot glass, then headed for the living room. As he passed a bookshelf, he withdrew the blackbound, typewritten version of Selena's diary.

Too bad he hadn't gotten a better glimpse of the thug Selena had met in the park. *She* might not look like a lowlife, but her partner was as short and stubby as the butt of a cigar and looked like a two-bit player in a mob movie.

Seating himself in an armchair, Edison glanced at the silver shoe he'd left on the table, trying not to torture himself with recollections of her slender feet. He opened *Night Pleasures,* flicked on an antique, glass-shaded oil lamp he'd recently wired for electricity, and began leafing through the pages.

More of the same.

This time, *mademoiselle* had managed to get lost in the woods on her way to the pleasure palace. A violent thunderstorm had hit, so as she ran, her once-fine dress became torn, tattered by brambles. Dirt-streaked petticoats clung to her wet legs, and when the dress ripped again, a corset was revealed. Because her chest was heaving with exertion, the corset's pink silk, criss-crossed ribbon began unraveling until only white eyelet ruffles covered nipples that were pelted by the driving rain.

"The marquis," Edison muttered. "Here we go again."

But this time, he was determined to crack the code. The guy Selena had met in the park had to be fencing whatever she was stealing from IBI. The CIIC had to be right about the diary....

Streaking through the woods, she gasped as the tattered dress bunched uncomfortably between her thighs. A garter flew open, then snagged on lace, but no matter how hard she tried to reposition her clothes as she darted through the forest, the garter kept catching. It chafed, wiggling against a spot so sensitive that the pressure should have been painful, and yet it wasn't....

If only she could stop running and fix her clothes! But what if she came upon vandals or highwaymen? Unsavory men regularly combed this countryside, mercilessly using women for their wild pleasures, and she shuddered to think of them finding her in the woods, all alone in such a disheveled state. No, she refused to contemplate how their rough hands might feel on her breasts, how they might stroke the smooth skin of her thighs....

Squinting against the pelting rain, she whirled around blindly. Where was she? Where was the marquis? Were there marauders in the hills? Biting back a moan, she thrust a hand down, desperately trying once more to dislodge the chafing garter, but the faster she ran, the faster it brushed the hidden source of her pleasure. Heat flooded her, along with a slow-building sensation she'd previously only associated with the marquis.

Edison exhaled slowly. As usual, her fantasies were threatening to get him aroused. Shifting uncomfortably, he shook his head to clear it. If he was going to decipher her diary, he needed to keep reading.

The rain pelted her, the strong wind working like fingers to finish unlacing her corset. Just as her breasts spilled from her dress, she saw light spilling from a doorway and stumbled toward it, her trembling hands grasping what remained of the fabric. But she had to let go to shut the cabin door.

Warmth from a fire hit her. And then a voice. "Ah. Mademoiselle Duclaire. I've been waiting."

She turned to see the marquis reclining on a small, iron-frame bed, slowly plucking juicy red grapes from a crystal bowl and popping them, one by one, into his sensual mouth. A sheet was draped across his hips. He'd dispensed with the ribbon that had held back his hair, and now the long, blue-black lengths teased his broad, bare shoulders. He looked so warm and wellfed that she couldn't fight the pure fury coursing through her.

"What do you take me for," she demanded breathlessly, "a serving wench? Someone who cares that you've been waiting for her in a warm cabin? If you were a gentleman, you would have come looking for me! I could have been attacked!

Your directions were poor, sir, and I got lost."

"I've no doubt that a woman of your disposition can take care of herself. Besides, you're here now, all in one piece," he countered, a slow, sensuous smile curving his lips. "Even if your clothes didn't quite make it."

"You care for no one but yourself, Marquis!" she exclaimed hotly. And for that, tonight, she'd wield her female power. "You won't be having me, not even if you try until dawn."

He deliberately misunderstood. "I'll be enjoying you until dawn?"

"I said you'll hear the cock crow, sir."

"Ah," he murmured, "hear the cock. And so shall you," he assured her. With devilish lights dancing in his eyes, he tossed back the sheet. As he moved lithely from the bed and playfully circled her, she tried not to react to his nakedness, but it was impossible. His finger caught a last wisp of pink silk ribbon. "My clothes!" she exclaimed furiously, intending to reprimand him.

"Indeed," replied the marquis as they fell to the floor.

His chest tight, Edison pictured the blazing fire, the cramped room, the waiting bed. But now he and Selena were the players. His eyes dropped slowly over breasts he'd already seen and touched and kissed. One at a time, he lifted them, palmed them, tested their weight. They tasted as good as... There were no words, he decided, but his waiting mouth fell on them, his tongue circling—

"Enjoying yourself, Lone?"

Rearing his head back, he was simultaneously conscious of three things: one, Selena was in his house; two, she'd appeared from the shadows near a bookcase; and three, he was aroused, just as he always was whenever she was around.

She pretended not to notice as she stepped into the dim light emitted by the converted oil lamp, her tight black stretch pants and skin-hugging black top setting off her pale skin. She'd changed clothes since he'd seen her in the park with her partner. Whipping off night goggles, she tossed them next to the diary and her shoe, then soundlessly dropped a tool belt, from which hung the equipment she'd used to break in. After that, she tossed her head in a stunning female display, sending a curtain of thick, glorious red-gold hair swirling around her shoulders.

Her eyes latched on to the shoe. "Prince Charming," she said. "Cute." Then she stared down at the diary, and because she was standing close enough to read the words, it was clear she knew what it was. Looking furious, she made a point of slowly dragging her eyes over his jeans. "Enjoying yourself?" she repeated.

"Very much," he assured her in a calm tone meant to unnerve her, still wishing M had barked a warning. "How'd you get in? I've got the security of Fort Knox."

"So do I," she returned. "But that didn't stop you."

Raising an eyebrow, he said casually, "You're right, it

didn't." He shook his head, offering a conciliatory shrug. "It's a cruel world we're living in."

"My sentiments exactly."

Since she'd gotten in here, she was obviously a trained professional. "I see that you're here. Where's my dog?"

"M's in the kitchen." Stepping closer to the table, she set down a shot glass she'd brought from the kitchen. "Eating the rare filet I was kind enough to bring him."

"Yeah," he replied. "You're a real sweetheart."

"Thanks." She poured herself a measure of whiskey, tossing it down like an ace.

He wasn't proud of it, but right about now, he'd have paid money to see her sputter. "Help yourself," he murmured dryly.

She merely lifted the bottle. "Care for another shot?"

Was she really offering him his own whiskey? "I'll pass. I try to save some for guests."

He'd meant to indicate she wasn't one, but she simply said, "Appreciate it," then poured herself another shot, obviously trying to get a rise out of him. Not that she could—at least he didn't think so, until she glanced his way again. The angry warmth of her eyes did strange, crazy things to his heart, which swelled with a longing he knew he had to deny.

"You bastard," she whispered huskily, her voice catching with something more than just the liquor. "You read my diary."

"We already established that."

"You really are a bastard," she whispered again,

those heartstopping golden eyes looking wounded, as if he'd invaded the inner sanctum of her mind.

He guessed he had, and felt a twinge of guilt—not that he'd let her know it. "Bastard?" He shrugged. "I've been called worse. And by women I've known more intimately." So why did the curse bother him, coming from her lips?

"I'll bet you have," she snapped acidly, abruptly turning and striding to the other side of the room. Her bravado looked a little forced, Edison decided, leaving him hoping she actually felt a little jealousy over the mention of other women.

He stood, intending to follow, but wound up merely staring at her. In the tight black getup, she looked sexier than any woman had a right to, and every time he took in her lush mouth, he remembered how soft, damp and pliable it had felt beneath his. She paused, leaning against a bookshelf, and now her voice sounded impossibly neutral. "So, what did you think of my diary?"

No doubt she was wondering if he'd cracked the code. "From a critical standpoint, I'd say you're no innocent."

She wasn't feeling nearly as cool as she wanted to appear. Countless things were giving her away: the high color in her cheeks, the rapid pulse at her throat, the lack of fluidity in her movements. "At least I'm real," she suddenly muttered, the comment nonsensical, her voice sounding strained as she glanced at the bookcase behind her. Before he could ask what she'd meant, she challenged, "Is this how you spend your lonely nights?

With books? Fantasizing about characters? Don't you have anyone to spend time with?"

If she was hoping to bait him, she was starting to do a good job, but he kept his voice level as he circled the table and went toward her. "Maybe I thought I'd found her," he murmured when he was close enough to feel her heat and inhale her scent. "Maybe when I read her diary, I thought I'd found a woman whose need for passion equaled my own."

Her breath quickened with his increased proximity. "Found her?" The unwavering, assessing quality of her amber eyes set his nerves on edge. "Seems more like you were following her."

Lifting a hand, he curled his fingers around her arm, wishing she didn't feel quite so soft and warm and female. "Following her was my job."

Eyes he could so easily drown in widened. "Your job?"

"Yeah," he muttered, fighting the impulse to lower her to the floor, shed his jeans and simply enter her. "Which means when she turned out to be someone other than I thought, I had to walk." He was only vaguely aware that his eyes had riveted on her mouth again. Fighting scent and memory, he told himself that he only wanted her for animal relief, that her imagination and charm didn't even play in the attraction. Too bad he wasn't better at lying to himself. "For the record," he suddenly added, "I don't fall for traitors."

"Who said anything about falling?"

"The same man who said something about traitors,"

he answered, the gentleness of his tone belying his dark mood. Even as his flinty gaze held hers, he admitted he was falling hard, tumbling into the sweet abyss. He'd never be able to control whatever spell she was casting over him.

"Traitors?" She studied him. "What are you talking about?"

He sighed. Dammit, he trusted no one, never had. And he hardly appreciated how this woman was messing with his head. "Don't play dumb. I'm smarter than I look."

"Brilliant, in fact."

"What? You did read my dossier."

This time she admitted it. "Yeah. I've got a class B security clearance and access to sensitive files. It's not strictly legal for me to see it, but your dossier was easy enough to get."

He hated that she'd read the dossier, since it made him feel exposed; liked it, since he'd wanted her to know him. "Well, then you're already aware I'm a government cryptanalyst, not an English teacher. I was sent to Sensitive Data Entry to keep an eye on you, Selena. Or whatever your name is. People want to know what you're doing here. IBI's security suspects somebody's selling secrets."

She looked taken aback, as if the conversation wasn't exactly going her way. "I can explain."

Lies, he thought, his own emotions suddenly taking him by surprise, his heart aching. Why did he have to be drawn to the one woman who'd be sure to tell him lies? Why had he pursued her? "Your ID's fake. You didn't exist before 1982. And judging by the contents of your apartment, you're ready to leave in a real hurry. The CIIC—that's the Center for International—"

"I know who they are."

"Well, they know your diary's in code. That's why they called me in."

Her jaw dropped, making her look so infinitely kissable that he almost gave in to the urge. And then she emitted a sudden edgy laugh that ended abruptly with her merely staring at him. "Somebody said my diary was in *code?*"

Hadn't he just lowered his principles by sharing confidential information? "What's so funny?" he muttered, instinctively drawing her closer, his body aching as much as his heart. "I've wracked my brain, wondering how somebody who looks as nice as you got mixed up in this. Mind telling me?"

Sparks filtered through the gold of her eyes. "Mixed up in what?"

He glanced toward the table. "The diary."

"Are you suggesting there's something wrong with female fantasies?"

"Any female's?" he queried, tired of playing games. "Or just yours?"

"Oh, that's you, Lone," she quickly retorted, the color in her cheeks nearly scarlet, her eyes flashing. "Servant of God and country. Mr. Clean-cut. All mom and apple pie."

"Mom and apple pie," he murmured gruffly, hating

how she affected him, that he couldn't control the rough tenor of his voice. "Didn't grow up with either. You read my dossier, so you ought to know that." His midnight-blue eyes bored into hers now, as sharp as razors. Things were heating up, and he realized he'd been waiting all night to take her on. Hell, he thought, he'd been waiting to take her on ever since he'd first laid eyes on her. Vaguely, he was aware that she was taking something from a waist bag and unfolding it against her thigh.

"How's this for loving God and country?" she said. "Badge number 7348904," she continued, quoting the number from the gold shield she was holding up. "I'm undercover for CIIC. They never asked that you be brought in on a case, and now, if you want to get technical about it, I've got a few questions for you."

Over the years, he'd actually come to pride himself on his guardedness. Distrust. Watchfulness. They were good qualities in his line of work, but ever since this woman had entered his life, every moment seemed to hold surprises. He could only stare at her.

"We can do it informally," she said coolly, clearly enjoying the catbird role. "Or, if you prefer, you can call a lawyer and make a sworn statement."

His eyes narrowed, his mind moving like a hand catching at straws. He was trying to find a loophole. This just didn't make sense. "Wait a minute. You're really with CIIC?"

She nodded. "Someone's using classified ads in the free papers to find buyers for sensitive IBI information, most of which is being heisted from the Sensitive Data Entry department. According to log-on data, it seems that someone in your division has cracked into their database."

Was she crazy? "Someone from my division?"

"You're clean."

"*I'm* clean." He couldn't believe it. "You were sent to investigate *me?*"

"Among others."

"Such as."

"Your boss. Carson Cumberland. Newton Finch."

This woman was out of her mind. "I'd trust Eleanor with my life."

"CIIC isn't interested in finding character witnesses. Your opinions are your opinions, nothing more. I'm after hard proof."

"Okay," he said, sighing and raking a hand through his hair, feeling pleased he didn't sound as shocked as he felt. "You're from CIIC. But how do you explain the diary? What's that about?"

She considered his question for a long moment, the irises of her eyes looking almost black in the dim light. All at once, something in her expression changed, and she seemed more vulnerable, more like the Selena who was stealing his heart. "The diary," she murmured. "That's a long story." She stared at him, hard. "Did you mean what you said?"

"About?"

"About wracking your brain, wondering how a nice girl like me got mixed up in all this?"

His hand gentled on her arm, and almost against his will, he found himself rubbing a slow, soft circle on the black fabric of her top. "Yeah. I want to help you, Selena. Or..." He paused. "At least I did. If you're with the CIIC, I guess you don't need help."

"Actually," she said, her tone conciliatory, "I could use some." Then she glanced away, the pulse in her throat jumping, this time with nerves. "I was nearly date raped in high school," she suddenly added.

The non sequitur was jarring. Before he could respond, she continued, setting the whole scene in a distanced way, almost as if it were a story she'd read that had happened to somebody else. It was just a sketch, the bare-bones outline of a near rape in the front seat of a boy's car. "And there were other factors," she informed him when she was finished.

Factors? She was speaking as if the feelings had never really caught up with her. And what did this have to do with her diary? Or her working for CIIC? "What factors?" Edison said, reflexively pulling her an inch closer and wrapping his arms where he'd wanted them for days, around her waist. "Selena..." His crazy, jangled up emotions were getting the best of him. "What happened?"

"I don't know," she whispered. "I just don't know." And then something deep inside her seemed to break—some resolve, a wall, a well of feeling. He didn't know what it was, exactly, just that she turned her head and gently pressed her cheek to his chest, and then words tumbled out quickly, urgently, as if she were in a confessional. She'd been tall and heavy when her parents had moved from Washington to the country, she said, and she wasn't popular, though she'd desperately wanted to be. She didn't go into details, but said the class president invited her to the prom, as a joke. After, when all she'd wanted to do was escape, another kid had offered her a ride home. On the way, he'd stopped his car on a dirt road and tried to rape her.

Edison felt as if all the air had left his chest. In his arms, she felt so fragile that he scarcely wanted to breathe. "What did you do?"

"Fought back. Ran."

Edison felt strangely sick. "That's good."

She glanced up, her eyes watchful, as if she didn't trust what he might do with all this information. "It was." She nodded, looking somehow lovelier than she ever had. "But I couldn't connect to men after that. Not like I wanted to. And I feel bad saying it now. So many worse things happen to women, but—"

Using his palms, he quickly cupped her cheeks. "But this happened to you." And he could kill the guy. But his mind couldn't catch up. She was from CIIC. And in the past somebody had hurt her. She trusted him enough to share that. Foreign emotions were whirling inside him, and he found himself wondering why love was always described as one emotion, instead of a thousand. Including murderous anger, since he'd kill anyone who laid a hand on this woman.

"My folks couldn't see that I wasn't popular," she whispered now. "And I never wanted them to. They thought I was so special. I never told them about that night...."

"You *are* special," he found himself murmuring, his heart feeling too big for his chest. She'd salvaged her wounded self-esteem and become an agent for CIIC. It was a hell of an accomplishment.

Her eyes captured his. "Thanks, Lone."

"No problem."

Still in his arms, she shrugged. "Last year, I went to counseling, hoping to get my love life on track, and the therapist I saw..." she swallowed hard, as if only now realizing how vulnerable she was making herself "...she told me to write down all my fantasies."

His voice was low. "Did that help?"

Selena ventured a little smile. "Sure," she replied. "I think I'm cured." More seriously, she added, "My feelings were hard to work through, but...I think I'm past them. Anyway, my mother found the diary. She sent it to a publisher, and I got an offer. Just as I was starting to edit the book, CIIC assigned me to IBI."

Gazing into her eyes, Edison found that work was the furthest thing from his mind. Leaning down, he bent his body into hers, enjoying how she felt through faded denim, enjoying how close she'd let him come, even though she had issues with men. "What's your name?" he asked quietly.

"Selena's my first name. I can't tell you my last. CIIC regulations."

"I guess I'll have to live with that," he muttered, his gaze flicking between liquid eyes and lips that he hoped wanted his kiss. "Last night, I wanted you more than I've ever wanted any woman," he found himself confessing, his words barely audible. "But because I suspected you were stealing from IBI, I felt I had to..."

"That's really why you..."

"Left you on the patio?" He nodded. "I've been going crazy ever since."

Tilting her head, she smiled shyly up at him, just as he angled his head down, letting his lips hover over hers, reveling in the intimacy he felt. "I thought you...didn't want me."

His heart was thudding hard. "I did. I do."

"I was hoping you'd say something like that," she murmured, lifting her chin a fraction to press her mouth to his. It was a sweet kiss. Silent. Assured. But just as his tongue flicked out, seeking hers, the lights went out. A crash sounded and, in the kitchen, M released two quick yaps.

6

"EDISON?" Selena whispered. Over M's barks, she thought she heard a footstep. She glanced toward the table where she'd left the night-vision goggles next to the bound copy of her diary, but with the lights out, it was too dark to see them. Curtains hid the moonlight and, outside, shade trees banked the house. Tilting her head, she heard M's nails scraping the kitchen floor as he gained traction, ran into the living room and under a sofa.

What had scared him? Or who? Edison's quick, barely audible whisper seemed surreal and strangely disembodied in the darkness. "It's probably a blown fuse. It happens all the time. It's an old house."

"But the crash?"

"M got spooked and knocked something over."

"Oh." Feeling the silent strength in Edison's body calm her, she squinted, hoping her eyes would adjust. "You have trouble with the electricity?"

"Yeah." But his voice remained cautiously low. "Just in case, did you reset the alarms after you broke in?"

"Of course. I'm from CIIC."

"I'm not doubting your competency," he assured her, "but..."

They really might have company. "I heard... something."

Edison cursed softly. "I hope it was M."

"Could be whoever's stealing from IBI. I think somebody's onto me. I thought somebody was tailing me in the park. Somebody," she added, "other than you."

Ignoring the jibe, he said, "How well do you know my house?"

"Pretty well," she confessed, the layout unrolling in her mind like a blueprint. "I looked it over the last time I was here," she added, though it was the wrong time to recall the explosive emotions that had come with his kisses. Ten feet to Edison's right, a door opened into the kitchen. From the threshold, the fuse box was within reach. If she edged straight backward, she'd be in the dining room. Through it, she could reach the front door and the stairs to the second floor. "We'll split up," she whispered. "You take the kitchen. Check out the fuse box while I take the front of the house. If somebody's here, we'll find them. If it's a fuse, you can fix it."

"It's a fuse," he assured her. "Otherwise, we'd know by now."

"Maybe not. Let's split up."

"No. You stay here."

She tried not to sound offended. "I'm a trained operative."

"You think I care?" Suddenly his breath was feathering her cheek like a fan on a hot, dark summer night. His voice was roughened by emotions as strong as the whiskey they'd drunk, whiskey that had made her mind pleasantly hazy. "I don't want you getting hurt, Selena."

Her heart fluttered. "I don't want to get hurt."

"You're starting to feel too important to me." A breath passed, a heartbeat. "Too many people I've liked have vanished on me. You know—here one minute, gone the next."

He'd said "liked," not "loved." Wondering if he'd ever break down and admit to needing someone, she edged closer, so their thighs touched. The words were out before she could stop them. "I won't vanish on you, Edison. I promise."

The low vibration of his voice rippled through her. "Don't. At least not before we live out some of your fantasies."

She smiled at the realization that he'd enjoyed her diary. Parts of her swelled at the idea of role-playing with him. "You want to play the marquis?"

"Absolutely."

On her shoulders, his hands were warm, big and wonderful. He'd read her wildest fantasies and wanted her; she'd shared parts of her past and he didn't care. He liked her for what she'd been, what she was now, and for all the things she wanted to become.

It was the wrong time, but a wall she'd hidden behind cracked like a mirror, and she could almost feel Edison pushing through to the other side, to a space she reserved for people she loved. Her heart stretched and she felt suddenly like a glass that was too full, brimming over the top.

As his hands cupped her shoulders and squeezed, she lowered her guard a crucial fraction. And then she heard a *tha-whomp*.

Strangely, she registered the sound first and only a second later the arc of air that came in the wake of a gloved fist. Edison veered sideways. His fingers uncurled from her shoulders, fell away, and his tall, lean body crumpled.

Don't breathe, she thought, whirling as he hit the floor. *Don't panic. Don't make a sound.* Her eyes strained into the darkness as her fingers fumbled at her waist, silently unsnapping the leather sheath holding her knife. As she withdrew the blade, she heard shuffling. Edison staggered up. Whoever was in the room with them was probably wearing night goggles, so she kept the knife pressed to her side, out of sight. Now Edison was silent again. They knew better than to speak and give away their positions.

Slowly, she edged forward, stretching her knife-free hand toward the marbletop table. Where was it? Had she gotten turned around? And *was* the intruder wearing goggles, watching her every move? Clenching her teeth, Selena tiptoed forward—until her hip slammed the table. *Ouch!* She was searching for her own goggles when another arching whoosh of air sounded behind her, where Edison still stood. *Smack.* She winced as she heard a fist connect, probably a hit to the gut, and then an all-out fight ensued. *Good.* At least Edison was still able to defend himself.

Forcing herself to ignore the smacks and grunts, she

tightened her grip around the knife and kept searching for the goggles. She had to find them! Maybe she could identify the intruders! She hit something hard—the lamp! It rocked, teetered, then crashed to the floor. M yelped as if hit. Glass from the shade sprayed onto her calves.

From behind her a hard driving rain of punches still sounded. Someone fell into an armchair; it's clawed feet scraped across the hardwood floor right before it overturned. A scuffle followed, a rolling tumble, more driving punches.

And then silence.

Selena knew better than to speak but, in that instant, she felt she'd rather die than live without Edison. Was he okay? Until now she hadn't admitted the depth of secret emotion she harbored. Raw fear was in her strangled whisper. "Edison?"

"Nope. That was the other guy."

"Music to my ears," she managed to reply.

But a voice as rough as sandpaper added, "too bad there're two of us. And now we know exactly where you are."

Her heart was pounding too hard, stealing her breath as she grasped the goggles. Pulling them over her head, she'd barely pressed them into place when someone grabbed her from behind. She twisted, but the knife was wrenched from her grasp. "M," she called as she fought to retrieve the weapon, "c'mere." M was small but had vicious teeth that would work wonders on her attacker's ankles.

A whimper sounded from under the couch as a strong hand suddenly yanked Selena backward, hauling her to a straight-back chair. Now she almost wished she wasn't wearing the goggles, for she could see Edison bound to another chair with twine, his head lolling on his chest, an eye blackened. Obviously, he'd lost the fight. Fury claimed her. "What have you done to him?"

"Same as we're doing to you," warned the sandpaper voice.

Viselike arms restrained her as abrasive twine was wrapped around her wrists, strapping her to the chair. She fought, struggling desperately to glimpse the other attacker. Her mind flashed on a dark country road, and, for a second the old feelings of helplessness threatened to engulf her. Biting back a powerless cry of frustration, she felt her ankles being lashed to the chair legs, then saw the other intruder. Like the first, this one was dressed in black, with gloves, a ski mask and night-vision goggles.

Duct tape was ripped from a roll. Was she going to die? Selena's eyes darted to the man behind her. *Oh, no! No!* she thought. *Oh, please, not now!* Not when, only seconds ago, she'd been contemplating sharing her deepest passion with Edison. "Edi—"

Tape was slapped across her lips, stopping the words.

As another length was torn from the roll, Edison tilted his head, slightly lifting his chin, and she got a better look at his blackened eye. Sickness soured her stomach. But he winked. And Selena would have given anything if he could see her answering smile. He was so smart. So sexy. So cool under fire. Clearly, he was faking injury, so they wouldn't bother to bind him too tightly. And it was working. Just as duct tape covered his mouth, two things happened: M barked and Edison slumped in the chair his head lolling to one side.

The man with the voice like sandpaper glanced toward the sofa, unaware that the tape over Edison's mouth was loose. "That dog's unnerving me. Let's get out of here."

The other voice was husky, undistinguishable. "Hurry."

"He's out cold..." The first figure nodded toward Edison. "You set a bomb in the kitchen, right?"

A bomb? Behind the goggles, Selena's eyes widened; the duct tape stifled her cry.

The other thug nodded.

"Well, since it's going to blow in—" checking his wristwatch, the sandpaper-voiced man headed toward the door "—six minutes, we'd better get out of here. Lone won't come around before then."

So, they knew his name. She'd been right in thinking this was no random break-in. But why had they come with a bomb? Did they want Edison dead, or had they known she was here, too? Which of them—she or Edison—was the real target? *Six minutes.* The words echoed in her mind.

As soon as the intruders cleared the door to the kitchen, Edison's head raised. Ducking his chin and repeatedly brushing his mouth against his shoulder, he managed to affix an end of sloppily applied duct tape to his shirt. Jerking his head he ripped the tape from his mouth.

"Selena," he whispered quickly, "I know your mouth's taped, but I've got to say this now, just in case there're no more chances."

She hummed encouragingly. *What do you want to say?*

"I think I could fall in love with you."

Her eyes stung, feeling gritty under the goggles. Edison was glancing around, straining to pierce the darkness, trying to pinpoint her location. *I'm right here,* she wanted to say. *I can see you. I promised I wouldn't vanish.* Fragments of his dossier were catching in her mind. So many people had abandoned him. She saw him as a kid, attending some fancy prep school, knowing he didn't belong and that the odds were against him. She saw this house he loved being blown to bits. Ducking her head, she madly brushed the duct tape on her mouth against her own shoulder, as Edison had done. She had to get free! *Had to!*

And, right now, six minutes did not seem like a very long time.

I THINK I COULD FALL in love with you. As soon as he'd said it, Edison admitted it was true. He'd never met anyone like Selena. She was totally unique. One of a kind. A cipher that he could spend the rest of his life trying to decode. He wanted to make love to her, play out her fantasies, help her heal from the things that had happened to her in the past.

"If we live," he murmured. Eyes that had adjusted enough to make out her shape now roved hungrily over her, and when he saw she was tied to a chair, his heart thudded dangerously. He'd kill the people who did this to her. To them. Silently, he continued working his wrist bindings, the friction burning, chafing his skin. "Six minutes," he whispered as Selena caught an edge of duct tape against her top and pulled the strip from her mouth.

Her inhalation was audible, so sharp that he felt it in his own lungs. "Are you okay, Edison?"

Relief filled him at the sound of her voice and, despite that a bomb was about to blow, he murmured, "Don't worry about me. How about you?"

Her voice was strangled. "I want to know about you."

"I'm okay." It was ages since a woman had gotten close enough to worry about him, and he was surprised to find it felt good. Not that he could dwell on the emotions. "We've got to get out of here."

"I put on the goggles," she reported, her words now coming in a steady, rapid-fire stream. *Good.* That would help. The emotions they'd confessed to while under duress definitely required further thought, but nothing would matter if they didn't make it out of here alive.

Still trying to loosen her bonds, she added, "They took my knife."

No knife. He'd been afraid of that. Squinting, he watched her crane her neck, looking around. "Are the goggles doing any good?" he asked. "Is there anything in the room we can use to get out of here?"

"Yeah," she said, breathless from the exertion of trying to free herself. "I broke the lamp."

"What?" he urged. "We've got about five minutes now."

"There's a piece of glass, part of the lampshade—it's lying on top of the diary on the floor. You probably can't see it, but the book's under the table."

"And the glass is on top?"

"A big shard. It's jagged. Sharp. It's right on top of the diary," she repeated. "Can you scoot your chair to it? You need to go forward six or seven feet, then left about two. If you can free your hands and get over there, you can use the glass to cut the rest of the twine."

Already he was rocking, using the chair's legs—front, then back—to propel himself forward. Cursing, he shook his head. "The chair's too heavy. And they tied my ankles to the legs. My feet aren't on the floor."

Her voice spiked, panicked. "I can't move, either. This chair. It's—"

"Forget about it," he commanded. There was no time to dwell on anything other than solutions. "Think," he whispered, more to himself than her, wishing as he worked the bindings that there was something he could do to get her out of here. He realized she'd fallen silent, too silent. "Selena?"

There was a scurrying sound as she began struggling again. Her voice wavered. "We're not going to get out of here. Is there a clock? Do you have a watch?"

"No, but I've been counting the seconds."

"How long do we have?"

"Four minutes, maybe."

"Four minutes!"

"If I could get my hands free," he muttered, his voice edgy, "and then get that piece of glass..." Watching her bend at the waist and bite into the twine circling one of her wrists, Edison felt his heart breaking. She was tearing at the bonds with her teeth. When she spoke, her voice was higher in pitch, insistent, and she was sputtering, spitting twine from between her lips. "M?"

Was she calling the frightened dog from under the couch, hoping he'd snuggle in her lap until the end came? Staying strong for her, Edison mustered a last shred of hope. "We're going to make it, Selena."

"M's under the sofa," she said senselessly. "I heard him run under there." She raised her voice. "M. C'mon. Be a good dog. Bring me that diary."

"Selena—" Edison didn't want to dash her hopes, but they couldn't waste precious time "—M's worthless."

A whimper sounded. Selena said, "No. He heard me. He's peeking out from under the sofa."

Did she really think M would push the diary to her, so she could get the shard of glass? "We've got about three minutes now. Give or take." Adrenaline pulsed through him, drying the back of his throat, leaving a metallic taste.

"Listen to me right now, you miserable little troublemaker," Selena began, using the schoolmarms tone that had worked on M the night she'd visited. "It's about time you began earning your keep. If you don't help free us, who's going to feed you?"

Another whimper sounded as M scampered toward Selena's chair, curls flouncing. She jerked her head toward the diary. "Get behind that book. Use your nose. Push it over here."

Uncertainly, M wagged his tail, then sat.

"The diary!"

With a yap, he leaped up, landed on all fours, then rolled over. After that, he hunkered down and extended a paw, as if to shake. He was running through obedience school tricks that he hadn't yet attached to the right commands.

"Please," she whispered.

M whimpered again.

Twine snapped, unfurling from a chair arm as Edison broke free. Using his free hand, he released the other, then bent over to untie his feet, but realized there wasn't time.

"We've got about two minutes," he muttered, suddenly swinging his arms, using them for leverage. With his calves still lashed to the chair, he dove for the table. Grunting, he hit the floor as M whirled, barking in alarm at the crash. Ignoring him, Edison shimmied on his elbows, dragging the chair as he crawled toward the diary.

"One minute," he muttered. One minute to grab that glass and cut Selena's wrist bonds. If they could free their feet in thirty seconds and clear the house in another thirty, they might live. Of course, for all he knew, he'd counted incorrectly and was a minute off.

"Good boy," Edison suddenly whispered.

By watching him, M had gotten the idea and trotted behind the diary. Hunkering down on his front legs, he did exactly as Selena had asked and pushed the diary toward Edison with his nose.

"Good boy!" Edison repeated as he pulled his shirt over his head. Swiftly wrapping it around the shard of glass so he wouldn't get cut, he crawled toward Selena.

"Thank God," she whispered as he sliced through the twine.

"Get your ankles," he instructed, cutting the knots around his own. "We've got one minute left."

She gasped in terror. "One minute!"

He grabbed her hand as the last length of twine fell. "Run!" Pulling her to her feet, he lunged toward the kitchen, lifting his briefcase as they ran.

"What's that for?"

"It's the classified ads I've been researching," he explained, barely sounding winded. "The same ones you're interested in. We'll look at them. Get to the bottom of this."

As they ran through the kitchen, he glanced toward the microwave just long enough to see that a bomb was rigged to the timer. "Simple," he said. But there wasn't enough time to deactivate it. Bolting through the screen door, they hit the patio at a dead run.

"We're going to make it," Selena said, her surprise matching his own as their pounding feet sprayed grass and dirt. Renewed panic laced through her as they reached the locked gate in the privacy wall. "Do you have the key to the gate? It's locked."

"Yeah." Pausing as he inserted the key into the lock, she wrenched around, looking over her shoulder. He swung open the gate. "Get going, Selena."

Why wasn't she moving? Turning, he realized her eyes were riveted on the cottage, her expression somehow both terrified and sentimental. He understood. It was his dream house, his slice of heaven in the city, and he'd worked his tail off to get it. "Selena," he urged. "C'mon. There'll be other houses."

"M," she whispered.

He was standing on his back legs, his front paws pressed against the screen door, his brow furrowed and eyes glued on Edison and Selena. He wagged his tail.

The bomb was about to blow.

"Dammit!" Edison cursed softly.

Selena's voice cracked. "No." She grabbed his arm. "You can't go back!"

Shrugging off her grasp, he sprinted across the yard, dodging bushes and gritting his teeth against the coming explosion. Reaching the cottage, he flung open the door. "C'mon."

For once, M came on command. Lunging, he leaped into Edison's arms, burrowing against his bare chest. When Edison turned, his yard looked like a football field, the open gate like a goalpost in the last seconds of a game. Standing beside the gate, Selena seemed to be a million miles away, unreachable, like the cheerleader every teenage boy wanted but never had.

But you've got her, Edison. She's yours. If you can make it back to her. Wedging M under an arm, he used the other to protect the dog's head. Then he lowered his chin, kept his eyes on Selena and ran hard.

The sound of the explosion was deafening. The screen door blew outward, ripping from its hinges with a crack. Wood molding splintered, and shards shot like arrows through a thickening haze of red smoke that stung his eyes.

As tears blurred his vision, he heard her voice. "Edison?"

He could barely see, but he felt Selena pull him and M to safety. *She can see because she's wearing the goggles, he realized.* "You're amazing, Selena," he murmured, wishing he could see her more clearly through the smoke.

"You know something, Lone?" Her husky voice came out of the inferno. "You're not so bad yourself."

7

"BECAUSE OF MY CONTRACT at CIIC, I can't divulge my identity without clearance," Selena warned, curling her bare feet beneath her in the driver's seat of the black compact. "So, before we get to my folks' place, I really am going to have to blindfold you."

"So you keep promising." Edison's voice was as hushed as the night and, like the night, it made her long for the warm bed awaiting them in her trailer. The farm was the perfect place to hole up and figure out who was after them. "I'd be more than happy to let you blindfold me now," Edison added, "but you seem determined to torture me first."

"Torture's good," she teased throatily.

"Then torture away."

As images of tying him up with a silk scarf she'd put in the glove compartment flashed through her mind, Selena glanced through the windshield at the deserted public rest area off I-79. Around a landscaped park that included a rustic building with rest rooms and snack machines, darkly silhouetted West Virginia pines shot into the starry velvet sky. Insects whirred, circling like loops of string around a lamp on a post, and the light shone down, bathing Selena's car in a yellow glow. It was cooler in the higher elevations, and past midnight now, and away from the rest area, fog hovered like a worried mother, its thick gray skirt swirling over the mountains.

Selena inched forward until her knee hit the raised parking brake. "C'mon," she chastised, pursing her lips in an uncharacteristic pout and returning to the torture at hand. "Hold still. You said you would. You promised."

"I haven't moved a muscle."

"Nice muscles."

"Thanks. Go ahead. Have at it, Florence Nightingale." Nestling his neck against the headrest, Edison studied her, his expression intent, the usually unbroken thread of sensual tension between them temporarily severed as M scrambled from the back seat over the brake column, explored the transmission hump, then leaped onto the front seat. Using Edison's jeans-clad thigh as a step, he braced himself against the window, pressing his front paws to the glass. "You just went for a walk," Edison reminded him.

Glancing over his shoulder, M wagged his tail hopefully before offering a short resigned sigh, hopping down and trotting to Selena. He curled into a fluffy ball beside her as she gently pressed alcohol-soaked gauze against Edison's swollen eye. "Funny," she said with a smile, her heart still warm from the things he'd said to her earlier. "You really look kind of sexy."

He winced against the sting of alcohol. "With a black eye?"

"You wear it well."

His voice seemed to move over her in lazy, dizzying swirls, like cigar smoke in a dimly lit bar, and even though there wasn't any saxophone music, there could have been. A soft predatory light came into his eyes. "Sexy, huh? As sexy as your marquis, Selena?"

Her pulse skittered as she imagined Edison reading the words she'd written. "Sexier," she stated, aware of his proximity, his scent. "You're alive. And he's just a fantasy. No," she added after a moment as she cut white adhesive tape from a roll and began bandaging a cut near his eye, "the marquis can't hold a candle to you."

"Judging from what I've read about the marquis, he doesn't hold candles for anyone," Edison remarked playfully. "He does all his best work in the dark."

"So true." She sighed, enjoying saying things aloud that she usually reserved for fantasies. "Anyway, you are gorgeous." Tall as a tree, lean as a washboard and strong as a prizefighter: the way each inch of him filled the cramped car made her long to feel his muscular body covering hers.

"You've only seen half of me so far."

So far. Inhaling deeply, she drew in scents of sweat, grit and pure male exertion that, instead of being unpleasant, left her giddy.

"Ouch," he whispered. "Did we really have to stop by your place and get that first-aid kit?"

"Yeah. Besides, I needed my diary, and you needed a shirt."

"Since we left my car in Washington, maybe whoever tried to kill us won't realize we're still alive."

"At least not for a while. They might come after us again, though."

Glancing down, Edison took in the oversize black T-shirt he was wearing. "I definitely didn't notice this shirt when I went through your things," he said, shooting her a smile, just a white flash of teeth in the dark. "The shirt smells like you."

"I sleep in it." Watching his broad chest rise and fall, she doubted she'd ever enjoyed anything as much as this charged banter. "What do I smell like, anyway?"

Tugging her elbow, he brought her closer, his lips touching her neck. "Heaven."

Chuckling, she affixed a final piece of tape to the gauze and leaned back, studying her work. "How did you get into my place, anyway? My security's great."

"So's mine. How'd *you* get in?"

"I asked first."

"I asked second."

"I'm a girl."

"Woman."

She felt heat warm her cheeks, and suddenly imagined his arousal as he read her diary. "The way you probably lingered in my panty drawer," she teased, speaking lightly, as if the idea wasn't making unseen parts of her ache, "you'd never have noticed something so practical as a T-shirt, anyway."

He smiled easily. "You got that right."

When their gazes meshed, her expression sobered.

She had so many questions. Who was trying to kill them and why? And where was this relationship taking them? To bed? To broken hearts? To the altar? When she spoke again, her already soft voice was muted by the heater's hum. "Maybe we're just...excited," she murmured. "Just feeling a rush of exhilaration because we had a close call."

"No maybe. I'm definitely excited." Lifting a finger, he brushed curling strands of hair from her forehead. Arranging them against her cheek, he tenderly traced her jaw, his finger feeling silken. As she tossed the gauze and tape to the dashboard, he added, "You and I were survivors long before tonight, Selena."

Now he was talking about how they'd felt growing up, and color suffused her cheeks again. On the drive, she'd told him more about her high school days, about being overweight and living in a town where she hadn't fit in. Now caring and desire surged inside her, feelings she could only hope he'd never take advantage of. "We *were* survivors, weren't we?"

He nodded. "We've got that in common."

Her breath catching, she placed her hands on his shoulders, molding her palms over them, enjoying the strength in his body, the raw power. "I guess we deserve a little exhilaration, huh?"

Threading a hand deeply into her hair, he massaged her scalp as he drew her nearer. "We deserve everything good."

"Nothing bad," she whispered, bringing her lips to his as his tracing finger dropped to her chin. His dark blue eyes were intent, as if whole empires might rise or fall on the strength of whatever she was about to say next. But she only shook her head.

Need for her was in his voice, making it deeper, honey-drenched and thick. "What's bothering you, Selena?"

She shrugged, unable to tear her eyes from his. Now, more than ever, he was throwing her off balance, making her feel as if she'd just started a very long journey that wouldn't end until they were naked together. "It's just..." His words were still playing in her mind. *I think I could fall in love with you.* "I was just thinking about the explosion. Everything happened so fast...."

The dark slashes of his eyebrows furrowed, and then his face rearranged itself like a cloth from which the wrinkles had just been shaken. Slowly, he murmured, "You think I said what I did because I thought we were going to die?"

Now it sounded silly. "Yeah."

"I didn't think we were going to make it," he admitted. "But I don't cave under pressure, Selena. And I work with words, which means I'm careful with them. I don't say things I don't mean."

She considered a long moment, knowing it was time to start risking her heart. "I feel the same way about you."

He angled his head down and savored a hot, wet kiss. Then he said, "Like...?" He wanted to hear her say it.

"Like maybe I could fall in love with you."

"I like the sound of that."

"Lust would be good, too," she added.

"I don't know about you," he replied huskily, "but I'm feeling plenty of it at the moment, and given the heat we seem to generate, I guess I figured that went without saying."

"I want to hear it, anyway."

"Well then, as soon as we're near a bed, I promise we'll make love, Selena." He traced her lips with his tongue. "How's that?"

"Perfect."

The car had bucket seats, and the raised emergency brake dug into her thigh, but she'd never felt more comfortable than when he circled an arm tightly around her and pulled her to his chest again. When her lips found his, she couldn't believe the pliant strength that came with the slow pressure of the kiss, nor how the exploration of his skillful tongue had her breasts swelling inside her bra. Sinking against him, she sighed, feeling half-tortured by how bothersome the lace cups felt, chafing against the taut, sensitized tips. Only his well-muscled chest pressed against her brought relief, and yet that relief, in turn, sent heat arrowing between her legs. At the sensual stirrings, she bit back a moan and brushed her fingers over his shirt, tracing the silken hairs tangling beneath the cotton. She whispered, "We could make love now, Edison. Right here. In the car."

"I appreciate the sentiment. But the first time—" his voice grew hoarse "—I want to be in a bed, Selena. No gearshifts. No dog. No holds barred. Just you and me, and a real long night ahead."

I can't wait. Her voice catching, she said, "Do you think we'll figure out who's after us?"

His hand rubbed down her back, the splayed fingers spanning her spine, gliding over her slacks, seductively molding the contours of her bottom. "We'd better," he murmured, the rumble of his voice a tangible thing that she could feel beneath her fingertips. "Otherwise, we'll be stuck in hiding. Not that there's anywhere I'd rather be than hiding with you." He paused, stroking her hair, finger-combing it and arranging it on her shoulders. "Have you really been watching my boss?"

"CIIC's been watching everybody."

"But Eleanor in particular?"

"More than most. Carson and Newton aside, she's got access to the most information." Resting her head on his chest, Selena lifted her chin a fraction, just enough to study his pensive expression, how his eyes had narrowed to formidable slits, how his heavy black brows knitted. A tousled hank of raven hair fell across his forehead when he shook his head. "I don't know, Selena. I've worked for Eleanor a long time...."

She frowned up at him, wondering if it was her imagination or if he was witholding something. "And? Is there something you're not telling me?"

He considered a moment too long, then shook his head. "No. It's just that I know Eleanor. She'd be the last person to steal. They recruited her straight out of college, and she's patriotic, committed. Besides, she just got married."

"Married people can't be thieves?"

"She's happy. She's acting like a newlywed."

Selena could swear he knew more. "What about her supervisors? Carson Cumberland and Newton Finch?"

"I can't vouch for them. They were in on the meeting where I was asked to decipher your diary, though. At the time, I thought maybe it was a ploy to distract me from those classified ads."

Selena was watching him carefully. "So, you suspected someone at that meeting was up to something?"

He shrugged. "I don't know. It was just a fleeting thought. I didn't dwell on it."

"But you'd definitely vouch for Eleanor?"

"Yeah."

When he glanced away quickly, she decided she was foolishly letting her general distrust of men interfere with business. Shrugging off the feeling, she continued, "I've followed Eleanor. She's been taking circuitous routes to travel agencies. Maybe she's about to skip town." She sighed, suddenly rubbing her aching neck. It had been a long night. It felt like years, not hours, since she'd met Dean in the park. If she had a cell phone, she'd call him, since he'd definitely want to know the latest developments. Now she'd have to call him from the farm.

"Selena," Edison said, "there's a quantum leap between visiting travel agencies and starting a new life in another country. Besides, Eleanor takes a blowout trip every year. When she gets back, she has a dinner party with a slide show. Since I met her, she's been to Kenya, Bali, Portugal, Aruba...."

Gazing at him, she considered. "You're probably right." Reaching, she slid her fingers into thick jet hair that was both coarse and yet infinitely soft, and she nuzzled her forehead against the curve of his neck. "I never thought I'd feel like this," she murmured.

He hugged her closer, not seeming the least bit jarred by the change in topic. "Like?"

She shrugged again. "Like I said, I just hated high school so much. I was such a geek. It sounds stupid to say it now, but being unpopular, feeling unattractive and being shy was awful, especially since we lived in such a small town."

"It's hard outside small towns, too."

She knew he was thinking of how he'd felt as a scholarship boy in prep schools he couldn't afford. Her heart welled. "People can be so cruel," she whispered.

"Because they feel small inside," Edison said. "They don't know how else to build themselves up, except by putting others down."

Tears, hot and unexpected, pushed from behind her eyelids, and she felt strangely panicked. "Look, Edison," she suddenly murmured. "I don't really know what I'm doing here."

He frowned, still stroking her hair. "Here?"

"With you."

He looked slightly surprised. "What's wrong with me?"

"Nothing." Her heart missed a beat. "Just don't hurt me, Edison. Promise?"

His eyes captured hers. Softening, they seemed to melt into the night. "Don't vanish on me."

"I won't."

Everything around them was silent, save for frogs, crickets and the heater's hum. After a long moment, she huskily said, "Well, I guess I'd better blindfold you now."

His encouraging smile was heart-stopping. "Please do."

"I picked up a scarf at the apartment," she said, excitement coursing through her as she leaned over his knees and took it from the glove compartment.

"Red," he commented.

"I hate to cover eyes this gorgeous," she admitted, though he didn't seem to mind her knotting the silk behind his head. "The drive's not much longer."

"What about a kiss, *mademoiselle?*"

She sighed. For so long, she'd dreamed of a man who could traverse the slow stages of increased physical comfort with her. A man who'd enjoy every dizzying step from ground zero to full penetration. A man who would kiss, then fondle, then let her get accustomed to him in a way calculated to make sex perfect. "A quick kiss," she whispered.

"I don't know about quick." His hands glided down her arms, causing heat to coil in her belly. Giving in to impulses she couldn't fight, she shifted her weight, stretching a leg over his strong thighs, her eyes on the secured blindfold as she straddled him. He sucked in a breath, his fingers pausing, on the way to her waist, to trail down her breasts. Grasping her hips, he urged her more firmly into his lap.

He was partially aroused, and she gasped. Her mouth slanted sideways across his, her lips dragging languidly back and forth. The first kiss was slick and damp, the second wilder. By the third, it was like water in a drought or fire in an igloo. As the slow hungry thrust of their tongues turned rhythmic and demanding, her hips ground against him, seeking him. His fingers closed over a breast, then plucked the tip through her shirt.

"Ah...Selena." The quickening of his breath swept through her like fire. "I've wanted to touch your breasts again, ever since that night on the patio."

Everything about her felt ragged—her nerves, her voice. "You are...touching me." And the circular, rolling movements of his fingers were both bliss and torture. She suddenly flung back her head, riding him, loving him with their clothes still on, whimpering from the pleasure.

His voice, just like his body beneath his zipper, was extremely strained. "There really is a bed where we're going, right?"

Her voice hitched. "A big one."

Thrusting a hand beneath her hair, he grasped her nape, dragging her head away, so that she was looking at him. With the red scarf still obscuring his gaze, he was her dream image of the marquis, coming from the masked ball.

"A bed," he said. "I want you in it, Selena."

She was watching his lips move, knowing hers were about to claim them again. "Soon," she promised.

And then she leaned forward once more, delivering a kiss that topped all those in her fantasies, lightly tracing his mouth with the tip of her tongue, licking his lips as if they were the sweetest cream she'd ever tasted. She kissed him until they were both lost to the pleasure...and until he suddenly moaned deeply, his strong fingers tightening. With a slow, heartfelt grin, she realized she'd made him come right there in her car, in his jeans.

8

"SO, YOU REALLY CAN'T tell us why you've come so unexpectedly?" Selena's mother, Annie, prompted. She was padding barefoot toward a planked oak table she'd covered with newspapers, and as she set down a platter of crab legs, her long sundress, fashioned from silk neckties, swirled around her calves. Seating herself on a bench next to her husband and across from Edison and Selena, she added, "Babe, are you sure everything's fine?"

Jerry had been humming a Crosby, Stills, Nash and Young song. "Are you *sure* you're not in trouble, Babe?"

Edison bit back a smile as he gently squeezed Selena's knee under the table. *Babe.* The way Selena's parents tagged the endearment onto every sentence, he was sorely tempted to start humming the Sonny and Cher song.

"No." Reaching for a crab leg, Selena cracked open the shell, prompting everybody else to serve themselves. "Edison and I...are, uh, friends, and we just wanted to get out of town for a few days."

Jerry didn't look convinced.

Pregnant. That's what Edison figured Selena's father

was thinking. With that came the sudden idea that Edison really *could* get Selena pregnant, and he was surprised to find he didn't mind the notion. Even though he hadn't felt this scrutinized since he'd applied for his class A security clearance at IBI, he offered the other man a frank, friendly smile.

An honorable person. That was his first impression. Jerry was tall and wiry, with an angular, chiseled face and intelligent amber eyes just like Selena's, though his peered from behind round wire-rims. While Annie's hair was in the style of a bygone era, its straight, waist-length strands as white-silver as the moon, Jerry's was identical to Selena's in color and texture. Not to mention length, Edison mentally added, since the ponytail hanging down the man's back was long enough to bisect the Save the Whales logo on the back of his T-shirt.

"Okay, Dad," Selena finally conceded. "We came because of something work related, but we can't go into details, okay?"

"Top secret," Edison added, with a chuckle meant to ease her parents' concerns. He was fairly certain they didn't know how dangerous their daughter's work could get, and despite their "do your own thing" attitude, Edison suspected Annie and Jerry would lock Selena up tighter than a drum if they had any inkling of last night's brush with death.

"Don't pressure them," Annie softly admonished her husband, sliding some crab claws onto Edison's plate. "Edison's a guest, remember?"

Jerry looked appalled. "Am I pressuring? We want you to feel at home. Any friend of Selena's..."

"Don't worry," Edison assured them. "I can take a little scrutiny."

Jerry lifted his hands, palms out. "I just thought you kids might have come here to talk."

"The kids are thirty," Annie pointed out with airy laughter.

Selena nodded toward Edison. "Thirty-five."

Fortunately, Jerry didn't seem to mind a little laughter at his expense. "Well," he murmured philosophically, "kids never really grow up, do they?"

"Sure we do," countered Selena. "But you got stuck in a time capsule." She grinned wickedly. "Along with Neil Young and the Grateful Dead."

"You like Neil Young," her mother reminded her.

"Hip huggers are back in style," added Jerry. "Platform shoes, too."

"I haven't bought any. And wearing socks with Birkenstocks sandals is still a fashion no-no," warned Selena, sending a pointed glance toward her father's feet.

"See?" murmured Jerry good-naturedly, shaking his head as he lifted another crab leg from the platter. "This is what happens if you encourage open communication with children."

Glancing around as the banter continued, Edison decided it would be impossible not to like Annie and Jerry, and yet he understood why Selena hadn't approached them with some of her more painful life experiences, despite their openness. The couple had survived into middle age without losing their naiveté or the rare charm of youthful idealists, and this farm was the embodiment of their ideals. Edison figured Selena hadn't wanted to see them hurt on her behalf. They'd clearly been good parents, though. They possessed a sense of social responsibility and political passion, and while Edison figured he wouldn't see eye-to-eye with them on all the current issues, he responded to the passion.

No, he thought as he dipped succulent white crab meat into a tiny pot of melted butter, not many people committed their lives to making the world a better place. Quite simply, it felt good to be here.

It had been nearly dawn when he and Selena parked under a weeping willow and hiked up the hill to her trailer, and while he'd had every intention of making love to her last night, they'd both been too exhausted. It was the first time in his life Edison had ever shared a bed with a woman without having sex, and when he'd awakened late this afternoon to find her dressed and visiting with her folks, he was glad. Sleepily, he'd savored the memory of holding her, of how warm and pliable she'd felt lying in his arms, wearing only a T-shirt. For the first time, he'd understood what it might be like to share domestic peace with a woman. With Selena.

Now he stared through a bay window at the lush, hundred-acre spread. A sliver of moon was visible, hanging above the mountains in a sky the color of the pink roses Annie had planted beside a butterfly garden.

Spring leaves uncurled on the branches of dogwoods and redbuds, and the trees created an arbor, lining a dirt path to a decorative, scrolled iron gate and tumbledown barn. M was merrily chasing some grazing pet lambs.

"Very definitely a place where you can let it all hang out," Edison remarked appreciatively toward the end of the meal, just as he spotted another of the many gargoyles that peeked from unlikely places in the grass.

"We like to encourage creative energies," Jerry affirmed.

"Let your imagination be your guide," added Annie.

Sending Selena a sideways glance, Edison thought of her diary, not to mention how she'd gotten his creative juices flowing in the rest area off I-79 last night. He hadn't lost control like that since he was a teenager. She'd insisted on driving away before he'd pleasured her, which had only whetted his curiosity and appetite. "Very creative," he murmured. And then, as if someone might read his deeper thoughts, he added, "Selena's trailer, I mean."

As he cracked another crab leg, his eyes landed where the trailer was perched on the hill above them. It had bright blue siding, hot pink flower boxes and lattice-work trellises through which Selena had woven bouquets of artificial flowers. She kept the perimeter of her satellite dish ringed with white Christmas lights year-round, and a shapely mannequin's leg, clad in a red fishnet stocking, served as the pedestal for a wooden bird feeder she'd made herself. The trailer was the quirkiest home he'd ever seen, but it had charmed him, made him laugh and made him wonder what surprises she was going to bring into his life next.

Glancing up, he realized she was beaming at him, and his gut clenched at the power of that smile. She was gorgeous. A sloppy ponytail barely contained the thick autumnal strands of her tangled, sleep-tousled hair, and tendrils curled on her cheeks like licks of flame. Her face was scrubbed clean, poreless and perfect without a hint of makeup, and she looked younger, somehow, as if the trip to her parents had regressed her to the girl she'd once been.

But she was all-woman. Beneath an old T-shirt, she was braless, and a quick, cursory scan of her breasts was enough to steal Edison's breath. His eyes trailed downward, caressing where tight, threadbare jeans clung to her hips, and suddenly, he wished she'd get up, just so he could get a good look at her bottom.

She didn't seem to notice. "You like it?"

Hell, yes, sweetheart. "The trailer?"

Not knowing what he was really contemplating, she rolled her eyes. "Yeah. The trailer. What else?"

Plenty else. "A little more personality than the place in D.C." He smiled with the understatement, his strong fingers tightening around her knee, molding over denim she'd lovingly worn to white. "And yeah. I do like it, Selena. A lot."

For the first time, he realized she'd been worried that he'd find the outpouring of creativity here overwhelming. Under the table, he glided his hand up her thigh, his eyes never leaving hers as his fingers curled downward, casually tunneling toward her female heat. "It's great," he assured her, then glanced at her parents. "Really. I've never seen anything like this place. Everything's amazing, including the meal."

Annie glanced through an archway to the kitchen and living room toward the pictures Edison had learned had been painted by her art students, colleagues and friends. Nearby was an assortment of foreign musical instruments Jerry played and collected. "This place is..." she chuckled softly, "...unique to us, I suppose."

"But make yourself at home," Jerry quickly added. "Hang out. Do what thou wilt." He suddenly laughed, eyes so like his daughter's sparkling with amusement as they slid toward his wife. "We do have one rule, though."

Edison tried to look grave. "A rule? That sounds ominous."

"Yep," warned Jerry, using a thumb to push his wire-rims back onto the bridge of his nose. "If you want to shower naked in the waterfall on top of the hill, you need to forewarn us."

"Dad," Selena drawled. "Hold the free-love routine."

For a second, she sounded like the embarrassed teenager she must have once been, and Edison was shocked to find that it moved him in some deep, profound way. What must it be like to share a lifetime? To know, year after year, that people like Annie and Jerry were there for you? To never really lose the person you were as a child because someone else loved you enough to remember?

He had no idea. He'd never trusted people not to leave. It was why whenever he thought he might get hurt, he severed ties. He always told himself the lack of long-term commitments was a conscious choice, but even he was astonished at how readily he could cut ties and never look back.

Selena had reached across the table to playfully bat her father's arm. "There are some family rules you can keep to yourself," she said. "We have company."

"Company," teased Annie, licking melted butter from her lips, "who slept in our daughter's trailer last night."

Selena held up a staying hand, a slight blush staining her cheeks. "If we decide to run around naked, you two will be the first to know. Happy now?" She glanced at Edison. "Can you believe them?"

Before he could respond, Annie continued, "Edison may be company, but aren't you going to tell us what your hunky friend thinks of your diary?"

"Ah, yes," said Jerry sagely, his eyes alive with amusement. "The diary."

Selena gaped at her father. "You didn't read it, did you? You promised you never would."

Jerry turned serious. "No. I said I wouldn't."

"It'd be too..." she searched for a word "...*strange.*"

"Strange?" prompted Edison.

"To have your father read something like that," she clarified.

Annie looked satisfied. Eyes that were as silver as her hair shone with interest. "So, Edison does know about your fantasies?"

Selena sighed, exasperated. "Mom."

Edison tried, but it was hard to maintain a poker face when he'd enjoyed the erotic tales, imagining he and Selena were the players, not *mademoiselle* and the marquis. "I may have read a line or two," he couldn't help but confess.

Annie smiled. "Judging from your expression, it might have been a paragraph. Maybe even a whole chapter."

Jerry offered a mock grumble. "I feel so left out."

"You're pathetic," announced Selena. "All of you! One-track minds."

"So true," her father sighed, not looking the least bit bothered by the accusation. "And your mother and I aren't even getting rich."

"I haven't gotten rich," Selena declared.

"You will be when the diary's published," Annie said.

Selena's eyes zeroed in on her father. "Well, don't bother asking," she warned. "If I make it big, I'm not giving a dime to GreenPeace."

Jerry shook his head sadly. "Are you sure you're my daughter?"

Selena laughed, glancing at her mother. "Didn't we have an attractive mailman thirty years ago?"

Jerry guffawed. "No, you're mine, like it or not," he said with conviction, his amber eyes suddenly turning sharp. "She's my little girl," he murmured to Edison, "so—"

"Dad," Selena said, blowing out another sigh.

Edison barely heard her mortified protest. Instead, he felt the gravity of the moment, the love it had taken to build this haven in the hills, the energy this family had spent, creating such a special life. "She's fine with me," he assured them, emotion twisting inside him, feeling foreign. Strange, he thought. Selena had had all the love in the world, but she'd still gotten hurt. He'd always held out the illusion that love would be easy for somebody like her. His hand was still on her thigh, the flesh beneath feeling warm and alive, and as he squeezed, he wondered if he'd stick around this time.

She suddenly laughed, breaking the mood. "Thanks for trying to protect me, Dad."

When Edison's eyes locked on hers, he could tell she was pleased by how he'd handled her father, and he felt something he hadn't before, an excitement that was mirrored in her sparkling eyes. He'd gone on so many dates, taken so many women home. He'd invited them in for drinks, sat close to them on the couch, then moved to bed as if he was reading from a script. But he had no idea how he'd get Selena into bed. Whatever was happening between them was authentic. And that could get messy. Emotions were involved—hers and his—but he wasn't backing away. Beneath the table, one hand rubbed Selena's thigh; the other lifted a tasty piece of crab meat and dipped it into hot butter. He held it out for her. As her smiling mouth closed over his fingers, licking and sucking, he watched her cheeks pucker at the taste, her game expression lost as her eyes shut in bliss. "Thanks," she whispered when she was done.

Annie sighed once more, as if her maternal dreams were being fulfilled. "Anybody ready for dessert?" she murmured.

But it was clear he and Selena would be having dessert in her trailer—and that no food would be involved.

"COMFORTABLE?" Selena asked.

"Almost." Curving his hands over her hips, he spread his legs a fraction and shifted her weight so that she was firmly seated on his thigh, with both legs dangling between his. With a playful flick of the wrist, he tugged down the band holding her hair, then raked a splayed hand through it. "There. That's better."

Better? Selena wasn't so sure. Curling up with Edison in the armchair had sent her pulse racing into the danger zone. It didn't help that her parents had plied them with brandy after dinner, or that Edison had dimmed the trailer's lights. His bare chest was warming her side, while heat seeped through the drawstring pants he'd borrowed from her father. Swallowing hard, she thought of how explosively aroused he'd been last night in the car, and she considered turning around and straddling him again....

And he likes it here, she thought, her heart swelling.

Her parents enjoyed his company. And tonight... Her heart pounded doubly hard, making her breath painfully shallow. Heavy weight seemed to press down on her chest, as if Edison was already on top of her, inside her. Wasn't this the right time to tell him that every erotic fantasy in *Night Pleasures* was exactly that—a fantasy? That she'd never had a lover before? Or could she assume he'd already guessed the truth?

Strung as tightly as a high wire, Selena pushed away the thoughts, forcing her mind back to the issue—namely, figuring out who was trying to kill them. But it was hard to concentrate when she was in his lap, and when parts of her body she usually didn't notice at all were begging for attention. Inside and out, she felt so hot that she could swear her temperature would shoot the mercury right out of the thermometer.

Performance anxiety had made her suggest that she and Edison get to work after dinner. She'd said the sooner they solved the case, the sooner they'd be safe, and she'd begun riffling through the classified ads in his briefcase. Now, snuggling against him, she forced herself to read another one:

> Go around the world! SWF is a lover of many lands, and has traveled extensively in search of intrigue and adventure. If you want to know how it's done in foreign countries, I'm ready, willing and able to tie you up and share all the trade secrets I know. This wild woman has been able to study human habits from Hong Kong to Paris to Cairo,

while working for the government. Only serious high bidders need respond to Lover of Many Lands. Write with offers to any Washington newspaper.

She frowned. "Did you notice how they talked?"

Smoothing back her hair with a faraway look in his eyes, Edison huskily murmured, "They who?"

"Our attackers."

Tilting his head, he surveyed her, his eyes flickering over her skin. They really were gorgeous, she decided, the color of lapis lazuli and fringed with thick jet lashes that cast intriguing shadows on his cheeks. "I know I don't have any right to say it," he began, brushing a finger over her collarbone, "but your folks don't know how much danger you face at work, do they?"

Her throat tightened and she glanced away. "Of course not." And if the truth be told, she was starting to dislike the danger herself. "A guy named Bruce Levinson was sent into IBI last year," she suddenly added. "He wound up dead in an alley in Georgetown."

Edison's eyes widened. "Why are you doing it? You don't have to prove anything."

"I used to feel like I did. And my folks did raise me to believe that women could do whatever men could. Even if your job is to crack codes," she added, "you wind up in danger sometimes, too. Look at what happened last night."

"That's what I was thinking about. I'm worried about

you. And to hell with your CIIC contract. I know where you live now."

"I blindfolded you," she reminded him.

He stared at her as intently as if she might be about to vanish in that very instant. "Your last name's Stewart. It was all over your parents' mail."

"Somehow I don't think you'll cause CIIC a problem." She shrugged. "Last night, I figured I'd just bring you to the trailer, but when we got here, I wanted you to meet my folks."

"I like them."

"They like you, too."

"CIIC's got reasons for their policy, though," he murmured. "You need to be careful."

"Maybe I'm losing my edge."

"Then you need to quit." Looking disturbed, Edison gave a short sigh, apparently deciding to let the issues go without further comment. "What did you mean before?" he asked. "About the way they talked?"

Right before giving him a quick kiss on the lips, she teased, "They who?"

His grin returned, warm and devilish. "The people who attacked us."

"They didn't sound like thugs."

"How's a thug sound?"

"One of them said, 'The dog's unnerving me.' *Unnerving me*," she repeated. "That's not something a thug says."

Edison's eyes returned to the classified ads he'd been reading. "They sounded educated."

"Like white-collar workers, anyway," she agreed. "And only one was definitely a man. The other could have been a woman. All she said was, 'Hurry up.' The voice was low and husky, but..."

Edison draped an arm around Selena's shoulders, still looking upset. For a long moment, he simply read the classified ads in his hand, then said, "Back to Eleanor again. I know you see her as a suspect, Selena, but she's incredibly patriotic."

"But she went to all those travel agencies. And she takes frequent trips around the world."

"That doesn't mean she's stealing information."

"Where's she traveled?"

"I thought you'd checked her out." Before she could respond he added, "Like I said, Aruba, Kenya, Acapulco."

"I think your gut instincts were right," Selena mused. "Someone didn't want you reading the ads too carefully. I just wish Dean was around when I tried to call earlier. You say Newton, Carson and Eleanor all acted as if CIIC wanted you to investigate me?" She shook her head. "I just don't get it."

Selena followed Edison's gaze as he turned to look through a window at the glorious night. The liquid black sky was as dark as his hair, and, like his hair, it shone with light, touched by the moon. The sky was exploding in a stunning display of stars.

"The way I figure it..." Edison absently ran a hand along her thigh, eliciting a shiver. "Whoever was using those ads to sell IBI information needed to distract me, right?"

"In the meantime," she continued, "they had no idea I was working undercover for CIIC. Since I was editing *Night Pleasures* on IBI time, my diary came to someone's attention."

"Internal security red-tagged you," Edison agreed. "They're in Building Three. They review videotapes. Actually," he corrected, "they only view random selections, figuring they'll eventually catch somebody in the act."

"That's what Dean told me. It's not a very thorough way to go about things."

He shook his head. "Nope, but it's standard operating procedure."

"Anyway, since my diary was under perusal, whoever we're looking for decided to tell you it was in secret code. We've ascertained that much."

"And you assume it's Newton, Carson or Eleanor."

"I never assume," replied Selena. "It could be anybody who can give those three orders. It could even be someone at CIIC who has access to IBI computer systems."

"Like who?"

She chuckled. "My boss, Dean Meade. But he doesn't count. He wouldn't do something like that."

"But Eleanor would?" Edison arched an eyebrow. "Anybody else?"

"A few others could give the orders. There's a guy

beneath Dean who could have told your supervisors to distract you on the q.t."

"By telling me *Night Pleasures* was in secret code?" Edison's shoulders lifted with a rueful laugh that didn't meet his eyes. "It was such a far-fetched idea that it actually worked."

"Sort of," Selena agreed. "But you had your doubts."

"Did they really think I'd buy it?"

"No. You're too smart, and they know it. Which leads me to believe they're operating under a tight time frame, probably a week or so. Otherwise, they know you'd catch on and bust them."

"Which I will." His voice lowered huskily, turning as silky as the scarf she'd draped over his eyes the night before. "Though your diary could distract me far longer than a week."

She was conscious of him again, of his hard, hot body and the scent of spiced skin. "Fantasies are always distracting, aren't they?"

"Not nearly as distracting as reality."

Reflexively, her body tightened. Her skin tingled, covered with prickles, and her voice dropped to a soft rasp. "I'm distracting?"

"You bet. Selena," he murmured, dipping to nuzzle her cheek, "I admit it, I don't want to die. And we do need to work on this case. However, my powers of concentration are very, very limited at this particular moment."

Her own words sounded strangled to her ears, her voice cracking, her throat dry with anticipation.

"What's wrong with this moment? It feels really good to me."

"What's wrong," he whispered, curling his fingers on her thigh and repositioning her between his legs so she'd feel the power of his burgeoning arousal, "is that we're in the middle of the woods." He feathered a kiss across her chin. "In the near dark." He drew a sharp breath. "Alone in a trailer with a big bed."

"Last night," she whispered, desire quickening her pulse, "I believe you said you wanted me in that bed."

"Right now," he confessed, "I'm wanting that with a quiet desperation that maybe only males of our species can fully comprehend."

"You'd be surprised," she managed to reply, her words barely audible, the pulse jagged in her throat, her whole being consumed by raw passion and heady lust. "Women aren't stupid, you know. We comprehend quite a lot."

"Hmm. Females understand?"

She nodded. "*I* understand."

His eyes left hers, panning over a plush sofa strewn with pillows before coming to rest on a table, on her diary. He stared at the book. When his eyes found hers again, they were searing with purpose. "Are you ready for me, *mademoiselle?*" he teased gently, gliding his palm over the back of her hand, dropping his fingers between hers, then threading them together.

"Marquis," she whispered. "I was too nervous when we first got back to the trailer, but the truth is I've been waiting all night."

9

AFTER THAT, nothing was predictable, seamless or smooth—not at all as Edison usually expected while getting a woman from a living room to a bedroom. The clues he'd noticed—and withheld—in the classified ad had been jarring enough. Selena was right, he'd realized. Eleanor was a suspect. She had visited all the cities mentioned in the ads, and all were locations for major military installations.

Still worrying about that, he'd steered Selena into the wrong room—the guest room—rather than hers, across the hallway. Just as they reversed directions, Jerry called to check on them, and M leaped onto Selena's bed, whimpering to be let out. Because they were in the country, the dog couldn't go alone. Outside, while watching M sniff the bushes, Edison realized he was undergoing his first case of precoital butterflies. So much for male heroics, he thought, as he and M headed inside again. So much for being Selena's fantasy man.

Now he glanced around her bedroom, his heart aching as much as his body. She'd turned out the light, but opened the curtains to a sliding glass door, giving them a spectacular view of mountains and splashy silver stars. She was seated cross-legged in the center of the mattress, on a hand-sewn quilt, still dressed in her T-shirt and jeans, watching him expectantly, a pleased, anxious, somewhat uncertain smile on her face.

He couldn't decide what to say, so he settled on, "Hi."

"Hi." Her hands were resting on her knees, the curling ends of her loose hair sweeping her shoulders, and he suddenly wanted to feel those strands touching every place on his body that longed for her.

She whispered, "You're nervous, aren't you?"

Pausing at the door, he took a very deep breath. "Yeah."

She gazed up at him. "Do you usually get nervous, Edison?"

He shook his head. "Nope."

"I didn't think so." She said it as if she'd given his sexual background a lot of very serious consideration; in the starlit darkness, he couldn't see the color of her eyes, but he noted how they were shining, lit up with excitement. She said, "I'm nervous, too."

He wanted to defend himself, to say that things usually went like clockwork and that he'd definitely never taken a woman to the wrong bedroom before. But he figured she'd already guessed that, and maybe none of it mattered, anyway. All that mattered was how he felt. And how she felt about him. Thinking that, he found that his body relaxed. He felt horny as hell, but relaxed. Finally. He nodded toward the sliding door. "At least the view's perfect."

She giggled nervously. "Now that we found the right room."

"I was enacting your fantasies."

"My fantasies?"

"You know." He smiled. "How *mademoiselle* always gets lost."

Her eyes darkened, her smile deepened. Now she was watching him with pure unbridled lust. No woman had ever looked at him in quite this way—expectant, curious, anxious—and his heart did an unexpected flip-flop. He realized he really was scared as hell.

She was studying him. "I'm glad you read my fantasies."

Watching her, he thought about what he wanted—slow, deep sex that they'd remember for a long time. "I could recite them."

"Good. If we're going to enact them, it would be difficult if you hadn't memorized them."

Heat was flooding him, burning pleasantly through his limbs, into his extremities. "For the first time in my life," he said, emotion turning his voice gravelly, "I've got no idea what's going to happen in a bedroom."

"You don't?" He heard a twinge of concern.

"No." He shook his head. "Because I get the feeling you're about to love me with some honesty and genuine emotion, Selena." As he said the words, his heart was turning over and over inside his chest, rolling as if his whole body was a steep hill she'd managed to climb when no other woman ever could. God, was he scared. And hopeful. Yeah, he was that, too.

"In my fantasies," she whispered now, her eyes fixed on his, "they sometimes wear masks."

She'd said it as if that might help their flyaway nerves, and in a silence that seemed deafening, Edison could swear he heard the steady, rapid beat of her heart. "They wear masks," he countered, moving toward the bed, "but she knows who he really is."

"He pretends he doesn't care about her." Her whisper melded with the sound of the spring leaves rustling outside.

"Pretends," repeated Edison. "But he really does."

Selena's eyes fixed intently on his. "She's afraid he'll leave her for someone else."

"But she's the only woman for him."

Her gaze sharpened a notch, as if seeking to go further into him, deeper. "You're right. She wanders through all those rooms, and she always gets lost."

"He always finds her."

A heartbeat passed. Wonder seemed to touch her. "He does, doesn't he, Edison?"

"Yeah," he answered, the barely audible word curling through the room slowly, as airy as smoke, as he continued toward the bed. "He finds her every time."

Stopping before her, he stared down, and she whispered, "It'll be easy enough to find me, since I'm not going to hide."

The simple, honest words rippled through him as if they'd been injected straight into his bloodstream. They sent heat coiling through his limbs, binding up his emotions, so he felt he'd explode. He edged forward again, just an inch, now catching her scent in a room already touched by mountain air and spring flowers. His dark eyes perused her thoroughly, heating every inch of her skin, burning a slow, languid path he intended to follow with his hands and tongue. "What would your marquis do now?"

"Slowly take off his clothes," she replied, her breath quickening to a soft panting that fired his blood so much he bit back a moan. She hadn't even touched him yet, but she'd ignited his desire, and it was like a rocket, ready to take off and soar. "He'd press his tongue to my skin," she continued, the words nearly lost, spoken so low he had to strain to hear. "He'd swirl his tongue on my flesh. Want to devour me. He'd sear my soul, kindle it with longing that only he could fulfill."

"Damn, Selena," Edison couldn't help but whisper, his heart hammering so hard that his knees felt weak. "You definitely have a way with words." Pausing, he added, "And while I've never had competition quite like your marquis, I'll do my best tonight."

The shake of her head was so slight that nothing else—not the strands of her hair or even her lips—seemed to move. "I don't want the marquis."

He was a little worried, since he'd thought her fantasies were the key to what made her tick sexually. "You don't?"

When she shook her head again, the lights he'd noticed in her eyes looked more like unshed tears, and when she spoke, her voice wavered. "I want you, Edison Lone."

He was still watching her, his eyes even hotter now, like torches she'd struck a match to, his lips parting and emitting a sigh as she grasped the hem of her T-shirt and pulled it over her head. She'd been braless, and as she tossed away the shirt, a sheen of silver starlight played on her breasts, reminding him of how she'd looked in the dress she'd worn to Passer la Nuit.

And yet she wasn't in a dress. She was naked. This was her skin, bare and beautiful; her breasts full and pert, with waiting, distended tips the color of brown sand under the sun on the hottest day of the world's hottest summer. It was better than any fantasy either of them could conjure, and the moment suddenly seemed so damn real that it shook him to his core. He became conscious of his own response. He was full and heavy, the weight pressuring his belly bothersome now, uncomfortable. He wanted relief, but he didn't move. He'd never been so aware of someone's eyes studying him; hers were glazed and starry as her long, slender fingers flicked open the snap of her jeans, then dragged down the zipper, exposing pink silk panties.

Time stopped. For a second, he didn't breathe. Nothing mattered but her. The back of his throat went so dry it hurt as his eyes roved from the glory of her breasts to the pants she'd just opened in invitation to the succulent mouth he was about to kiss. Never taking his gaze from her, he tugged the drawstring to his pants, then glided both hands to his waist and slipped them inside the waistband. Moving just slowly enough to tease her, he pushed the pants over his hips and stepped out of them, then stood there in white briefs. Her gaze fastened *there,* where cotton outlined each blessed inch he had to offer. Shivering, he reached instinctively, clasped her hand and brought it to where he ached.

She whimpered, scooted closer, and he uttered something between a growl and a groan that sounded downright dangerous. Need took over then. He shut his eyes. His head rolled back on his shoulders in ecstacy, his hips thrust forward, his palm glided over the water-smooth back of her hand, urging her to tighten those luscious curling fingers around his thickness. And she did, moving them along the shaft. Once. Twice. Then he had to shift her hand away, hoarsely whispering, "I won't last."

When he opened his eyes, she was staring at him with such a combination of awe and lust that he felt tenderness he'd never guessed he was capable of. "Go ahead, Selena," he murmured, and although it took all his control, he let her push her fingers inside his briefs, wincing as she drew them down, exposing tender aroused flesh, her gaze alone pushing him right to the brink of release.

Quickly cupping her face, he brushed a thumb over the line of her cheekbone, then over her lips, his heart clutching, since he suddenly, illogically, half expected this precious moment to be snatched away. Deep down, he was sure nothing this good could ever last. Could it? Was it possible? "You do want me, don't you, Selena?"

"Oh, yes."

It was damn obvious how much he wanted her.

Leaning down, he touched his lips to hers with hard, hot pressure, feeling strangely raw, and sure that this was how a man was supposed to feel when he made love. Yeah, it was supposed to be exactly like this. Arousing as hell. Significant. Explosive. Whatever happened next, Edison knew he wouldn't dismiss her from his mind as soon as the last traces of sexual satisfaction had faded.

That was what usually happened.

But everything about this was a first, because Selena was doing something completely crazy to him. "Look your fill," he whispered. "Touch me all you want. Play out your fantasies. You can be anybody you want with me, Selena."

"I want to be me." She closed her fingers around where he was so thick, hard, hot. Huge and engorged, explosively tight, every inch of him her eyes drank in as she came across the mattress on her knees with her jeans half-off.

He was totally lost. "Selena." Gasping her name, he dug his hands into her hair. "You don't know what you're doing to me."

But she did. And before he could react, she'd lowered her mouth. He went blind. Or had he simply shut his eyes? Sucking air through clenched teeth, he realized his eyes were open and he was staring dumbly where her lips circled him, where the red-gold strands of her hair brushed his thighs. Shutting his eyes once more, he melted into heaven until he knew he had to draw away. Raggedly, he whispered, "I need to be inside you."

There was a breath—his. A pant—hers. And then he added, "Here. Let me help you with your clothes."

The eyes that found his were whiskey colored and drunkenly dazed with need, and if he'd had any doubt, he was now sure she was going to break his heart. The way she licked her lips, they could have been smeared with hot caramelized sugar instead of his taste. His heart stuttered. "You're still dressed," he rasped, urging her to lie back. "I never do this," he added, gently tugging the denim down the satin skin of her legs. "I always undress a woman first." The words seemed strangely futile. How could he explain that everything was different this time? He didn't even bother. Instead, his eyes trailed up the endlessly long, smooth legs he'd bared, stopping at her panties.

As good as she looked in them, they had to go. He got rid of them, then, gently molding his hands over her knees, he pushed her legs apart. "The idea is that the woman gets undressed first," he murmured. "She needs more attention. Foreplay."

"Edison," Selena said in a tremulous voice, crooking her arms on a pillow so that her dazzling hair spread over the pillowcase. "I wouldn't worry about it. I'm ready. I think we can forget foreplay."

Leaning forward, following her command, he delivered a deep, wet tongue kiss. Hands greedily found her breasts and, in doing so, warmed the rest of her. His mouth locked over a nipple. Sugar and salt assaulted his taste buds as he suckled, pulling shuddering cries from her.

By the time she was senselessly calling his name, he barely heard. There were too many sensations. Moonlight and shadows dancing on creamy breasts that were turning feverish under his hands, the skin moist as if she'd sprinted through a spring rain. Musk that filled him as his lips fastened more tightly around a taut bud, the aroused length of him sliding against her thigh. Her hips started seeking his with hot, primal rhythm, and her voice came in high cries.

"Selena?"

She moaned, and that was enough. Her soft pants and gasps had him settling between her legs, moaning once more himself when he felt her open, wet heat. Until now, he'd never known how much he needed her, how much he needed so many things. Love, he thought, incoherently. He needed that. He'd do anything for it.

She was moving beneath him, her breath quick, her hips lifting, straining, as his lips captured hers in another possessive kiss. Suddenly, she took his hand, dragged it down from a breast, guiding it between her legs, and as she did, the air seemed so thick with silence and sex that he couldn't breathe. He thought his hand was shaking, then realized the trembling came from her thighs, and as he deepened the kiss, his tongue plunging, he realized she was coming. He wasn't even inside her and she was gushing. No, she definitely didn't need foreplay at the moment. No woman had ever been so wet. No man so hard.

He quickly pushed inside. He flowed into her, burning and hard, molten and liquid, thrusting deeply, until he could go no farther, ready to spill. *Too tight.* A warning sounded in his head, coming out of the blue, as if from nowhere. He gasped. "Selena?"

Everything stopped.

He was aware of her panting breath, of his. Silver stars burst outside. Skin met skin from forehead to toes. His fingers curled, twining in her hair, and his cheek was pressed against hers. Blood was rushing in his ears, his heart hammering harder than it should have. Exhaling shakily, he tried to replay the past few seconds. As he'd thrust inside her, she was still having a hard, fast orgasm, the heavenly spasms of which were clutching him, but she'd been tight. *Too tight...*

"I should have told you," she whispered, trusting eyes finding his as she cupped his shoulders. "I've never done this before. But you said you were nervous, so..."

Not *that* nervous. He'd have wanted to know she was a virgin. Definitely another first. He'd assumed she wasn't very experienced, but he'd figured that somebody, somewhere, after that horrible night at the prom...

Licking his lips, he stared down at the face he now cradled between his hands. "Oh, Selena," he groaned. And then something strange happened to him, something he'd never forget. Love surged inside him, so strong that he knew there was no turning back. He'd protect her, provide for her. Do whatever she wanted.

Brushing aside a hank of hair that had fallen onto her forehead, he flashed on something else—a prom picture he'd seen as they were leaving her parents' place. All these years, she'd let them proudly display that gold-framed photograph on the mantel. Just as she'd said, she'd been heavy, taller than the boy, and in the picture, she was standing beside him, looking uncomfortable in a prom gown, trying to smile. Despite what she'd endured that night, she'd let her folks believe it was as magical as they'd imagined. She'd told them it was everything they wanted their little girl to have....

Staring down at her, their bodies locked in passion, Edison could only draw another deep breath, shaking his head. His heart stretched again with the need to make the present magical for her, make their lovemaking magical.

"I should have told you," she repeated.

"It's okay," he answered honestly, knowing he was already giving her his best. Even if he'd known, he wouldn't have been able to go any slower, or kiss her more deeply or more thoroughly. "Things are fine this way."

"Perfect," she agreed.

"Not quite perfect," he replied. "Not quite yet, Selena."

And then he showed her perfect.

Locking their mouths, he languidly stroked his tongue over hers, withdrawing and thrusting, his hips moving, each striving thrust delivering the perfection he promised. Each movement was a slow slick slide into oblivion on a night they'd never forget. It could have lasted hours, or only minutes. All that mattered was the unparalleled satisfaction that finally came when another of her climaxes rocked his world, followed by his own.

And within seconds, they were asleep.

"EDISON," Selena whispered, not expecting him to hear, not really wanting to wake him, but simply wanting to say his name. *I'm allowed,* she thought. She was naked, propped on an elbow, staring down at him. Yes, she was definitely allowed, after all the things they'd done tonight.

Not even her wildest, most private fantasies could match the pleasure of sharing herself with this man. And she would do so again before morning, she decided whimsically, sending a quick glance through the sliding doors. The stars were a shade paler, preparing to meld into the blue of tomorrow's sky. Soon pink fingers of light would reach down into the mountains, and leaves would turn silver-white under brilliant sunlight that would dapple the new grass.

But that would be later. Now it was dark. Quiet. Utterly still. Insects and animals had settled under rocks, or taken shelter among dew-damp leaves.

She stared at Edison again. He was breathing steadily, his body, like hers, well loved and relaxed. She took in the thick, swirling hair coating his hard, muscular pectorals, then how it arrowed down, thickening again at his groin, lovingly showcasing the most perfect male equipment she'd ever laid eyes on.

Not that she'd seen much male equipment.

She did, however, have an imagination. And Edison, she was sure, was truly spectacular. With warmth flooding her, she studied his high forehead, angular cheekbones and shallow cheeks, then the thick, jet eyebrows, the fringe around his heavily lidded eyes.

Her gaze settled on his mouth. It wasn't wide or lush or overly sensuous. Just a perfect, kissable shape that was now widening into a smile. His hand found her bare back and traced her spine. "How long have you been watching me?" he whispered, not opening his eyes, but sifting his weight so he lay on his back, his breath quickening as his hand drifted farther down, molding over her bottom. He reached for a breast, too, urging her closer for a warm kiss.

She pressed the words to his mouth. "I've been watching you awhile."

"And I didn't even know it," he murmured, his teasing voice low and husky, lazily curling through her blood. "Were you spying through the window?"

She squinted down at him. "Hmm?"

"Through the window of the cabin?" His voice rumbled, sounding deeper with sleep. "Were you watching me while I was getting ready for your arrival, *mademoiselle?*"

He was replaying her fantasy from the marquis's point of view, and it charmed her as nothing else ever had. "Getting ready for me?" she asked innocently, pressing the warming length of her body to his side and sliding her spread fingers through his chest hair, loving the way the silk pleasured her skin.

He nodded, lulling her into the story as if it were an erotic lullaby. "Yeah...preparing for you."

"What did you do, Marquis?"

"Lit a fire."

Selena chuckled softly. "Because you wanted me to get hot?"

"Very hot," he assured her.

"How hot?"

His palm continued curving around her bottom, dipping into the crack and then under, parting the cleft, pushing a finger where she'd stayed slick and ready. His words were touched with the heat he felt. "This hot."

Her senses reeled. "And then what?"

"I took off my sword," he murmured, rubbing a slow deep circle on her sex. "Took off my shirt. Breeches. Boots." His breath caught. "And then I washed some grapes, so I could feed them to you, one by one. They were so juicy...succulent." He sighed with longing. "But you didn't come."

"I was late?"

"And I was getting angry." Suddenly, he chuckled and rolled over, swiftly reversing their positions, so he hovered above her. Supporting himself on an elbow, he continued exploring the source of her pleasure, with his other hand. "Really angry," he murmured huskily. "Frustrated, as only aroused males can be. I'd seen all those women at the masked ball, wearing fine gowns, their perfume so soft and sweet, but I wanted you."

She shut her eyes, shamelessly moving her hips to the

rhythm he was establishing, her breath shallow. "And I was a noshow?"

Edison moaned playfully, as if he were a willful marquis who was about to die from unrelieved arousal. "And then it started raining," he continued, his voice growing genuinely urgent. "There was lightning. Thunder. I thought you'd lied. I thought you'd never come. I thought I'd never find you in my bed again." He slid his finger out and trailed a pattern between her thighs with his fingertips.

"But I was running through the woods," she related, her voice hitching, her hips twisting when he pushed a slickened finger inside again, exploring her. On its slow withdrawal, she managed to add, "I would have come earlier. But my garter came loose. It was..." Pausing, she felt heat flood her cheeks, spreading to the rest of her body. She'd written these sensual words, but the fantasy was so personal....

His voice, like his hand, was pure silk. "The garter was what, Selena? Tell me more. What happened in *Night Pleasures...?*"

"It was unhooked." Her jagged voice was almost inaudible. "Loose. Unsnapped. It was..."

"Bothering you here?" He flicked his finger against the place in question. "Like this?"

She turned her head on the pillow to face him. "It...hurt. Chafed. I was so mad at you because you were inside by the fire, where it was so warm. You were just lying there, eating grapes."

"And you were half-naked when you came in. Wet."

His hand was pure magic now, swirling and touching her more deeply than ever before. "So wet..." he murmured. "And your bodice hung open exposing your breasts. You said I couldn't have you that night."

Her words came on a throaty moan. "I said you'd hear the cock crow before you had sex with me, sir."

Edison's lips were in her hair then. And on her forehead, her cheeks, her closed eyelids. His kisses were soft, sensual, fluttery—a barrage of tender featherings. "The cock," he whispered between kisses, his soft chuckle thrilling her, since it brought the knowledge that sex could be what she'd always hoped: fun.

Skating toward another climax, she tried her best to sound stern. "Sir!"

"Hear the cock," he whispered, another playful chuckle sounding as his mouth covered hers once more and his hands bracketed her face. His aroused flesh now easily glided inside her, making stars burst everywhere he touched. "You said you'd hear the cock crow," he whispered again. "And so you shall, my sweet Selena."

Later, at dawn, a rooster really did crow on the farm, and hearing it, they cuddled closer together. With their arms wrapped around each other in the tightest imaginable embrace, they laughed until they found themselves making love again.

10

SELENA AWAKENED ravenously hungry, last night's lovemaking having burned up her caloric reserves, and she quickly decided that whatever wet tongue was lapping her nose, it definitely wasn't Edison's. The tongue was too little. Too sloppy. Too unskilled. "Cut it out," she whispered, her stomach growling as she opened her eyes to find herself confronting M—and the swift, startling realization that Edison was gone.

She shouldn't have known already. She hadn't yet checked to see if his moccasins were in the living room. Or discovered that his clothes had vanished from the bedroom. Or that the keys weren't hanging on the kitchen pegboard, and her car wasn't parked at the bottom of the hill. Nevertheless, Edison's absence registered deep in a body he'd loved so well during the night. Had his personal past caught up with him? Had their lovemaking scared him off? Was he abandoning her before she could abandon him?

The phone was ringing.

She registered that now. How long? she wondered. Was Edison calling? From where? Dragging the quilt from the bed, she covered herself as she jogged toward the kitchen. Where was Edison? Had something happened? Why, after what had occurred between them last night, would he have left her trailer?

He's not coming back.

The feeling came like a blow to the gut. Edison had left and he wasn't coming back, and what she felt for him was as irreversible as what branding irons did to flesh. "Don't be ridiculous," she muttered, trying to convince herself that her own fears and feelings of insecurity were at work. Just because she'd finally found a man to worship her body with erotic fury, and who'd wanted to fulfill her fantasies, didn't mean he was too good to be true. Maybe he'd taken her car and gone exploring, or into town to pick up some breakfast.

"Or maybe something happened to him." Her stomach muscles clutching, she snatched up the phone, terror in her heart. What if whoever bombed Edison's house had followed them here? She hadn't thought of that! Had they managed to kidnap Edison during the night because her own defenses had been weakened? After the fourth or fifth time Edison made love to her, *she* could have been kidnapped without knowing it. She just wished she knew who'd set those explosives.

Just as she registered that he'd moved the classified ads to the kitchen table, she realized someone was speaking. Her hand tightened around the phone cord. "Edison, is that you?"

There was a long pause. "Uh...no. It's Dean, Selena. I got a message you tried to call last night."

"I did," she said, disappointment flooding her. Her stomach growled at the same time and she realized she had to eat. If something had happened to Edison, she'd need her strength. She couldn't confront the guys from last night while fainting from hunger. Opening the refrigerator, she grabbed a colander filled with hard-boiled eggs and brought it to the counter, quickly cracking one over the sink.

Dean was talking. "It's a good thing you called last night. We've got a lot of new information. But why did you think I was Edison Lone?"

"Somebody blew up his house last night. Nearly killed us both. That's why I tried to call."

"You sure?"

She was losing patience. Dean hadn't exactly caught her in a good mood, and she didn't intend to tell him that Edison had just vanished from her bed. "Are you suggesting I wouldn't know when I'm about to be killed in an explosion? Somebody tied us to chairs and set a bomb. Does that qualify as *nearly killed* for you?"

"Sorry," Dean muttered. "Maybe you were the target. Maybe they were faking you out. Maybe they were going to let Lone go, after you were dead."

"After he survived an explosion?" That was another thing she disliked about Dean. He spoke a little too casually about things such as her potential demise. "I don't think so, Dean. Edison and I fled the scene together and came here."

She wanted to get off the phone asap, too, so she could find him. She braced herself, expecting Dean to remind her that breaking her anonymity was in violation of her CIIC contract. Somehow, she didn't want to explain that she'd tried blindfolding Edison. Dean would make something erotic out of it. It *had* been erotic, of course....

Fortunately, Dean stayed on the previous topic. "Then my new information doesn't entirely make sense."

"New information?"

"Yeah. Turns out Edison and Eleanor Luders have a history."

Trying to keep calm, Selena forced herself to ignore the horrible, sick feeling in the pit of her stomach. "Why don't you do me a quick favor," she said, her fingers now even tighter around the phone receiver, "and clarify 'history'?"

"Hot, steamy one-night stand," said Dean, not realizing that he was breaking a heart...a heart already so bruised that Selena had feared she never could give it to a man. A heart she'd given away last night, to Edison Lone. "They pursued other partners after that," Dean continued, offering information Selena could do without. "And afterward, Eleanor was instrumental in getting Lone transferred to her division. She really wanted him to work with her. Now two tickets to Bali have been procured, using one of Lone's credit cards."

Her heart hammered. "You're saying Edison and Eleanor..."

"Have been ripping off IBI together. That'd be my guess."

Edging toward the classified ads Edison had left on the table, Selena let her eyes rove over them as Dean continued, "The ads refer to places Eleanor's vacationed over the past few years, most of them cities with military installations. Not only has Lone been working with her, they were sleeping together."

"I think you already mentioned that." The pit of Selena's stomach turned to lead. "When? You said a one-night stand?"

"When they met. And yeah, it was only one night, according to one of their co-workers. Supposedly, it started after an IBI Christmas party seven years ago, then ended. But who knows what really happened?"

"Eleanor just got married."

"So?"

"So, if she's stealing from IBI, maybe she's working with her husband. And about her and Edison, seven years is a long time ago."

"Maybe whatever they found ran deep," suggested Dean.

Selena wanted to kill Dean. Edison, too. Not that she could believe his betrayal. No one was that good a liar. No one could love a woman's body with such sweet promise while planning to skip town the morning after with a tall, leggy, blond partner in crime.

But men had done worse. Hadn't previous experience proved Selena was a poor judge of character? She had never known Dean to make a wrong judgment call, not one. Realizing her hands were shaking, she glanced down and frowned. Blue ink had bled onto her skin from the unshelled egg in her hand.

She squinted at the egg. Printed on it was something

that looked like a letter of the alphabet. It was! The letter *I*. Remembering their conversation in Passer la Nuit, about how spies had communicated during World War II by writing messages on eggs, Selena quickly began cracking the rest. Some said nothing. Another said "you." Dean was wrong, she thought, her heart pounding. Edison was in trouble, and he'd left a message for her, a cry for help. But how, she wondered illogically, could he have stopped to boil eggs if he was being kidnaped or attacked?

Within seconds, she assembled the message: "I love you."

Her heart soared. Plummeted. Her mind clouded with doubt. Quite simply, she didn't know what to feel. How, under the circumstances, should she take this statement?

"They'll be on their way to the airport soon," Dean was saying. "I'm pretty sure of it. Which is why, before I called, I dispatched a chopper to pick you up and bring you back to D.C. It should be there within a half hour. You're the one who was sleeping with this guy, so you're closest to him—"

She was so appalled she didn't hear the rest. Didn't Dean realize she had emotions? What kind of robot did he think she was? Did he really think she'd slept with Edison to help CIIC solve a case? He was still talking. "So you might be able to get close to Lone again, Selena. If his place blew up, the way you said, then they're probably at Eleanor's house. It's a gated mansion in Arlington. Find them and pick them both up. Maybe whoever attacked you two last night was an unsatisfied customer of theirs or something."

If Edison really was involved with Eleanor, Selena knew she couldn't handle it. "Somebody else has to do this, Dean."

"I need to know you haven't lost your edge."

"And my arresting Edison will prove it?"

"If he's guilty, I want you to bring him in."

Truthfully, she wasn't sure she could. Even if he'd betrayed her, she'd want to turn a blind eye, not that she would. But she couldn't handle that he'd slept with Eleanor. And she didn't care if the affair had occurred as far back as the ice ages.

I love you.

Yeah, right. The words were probably about as sincere as Brent Enderwood's invitation to the Stars of Tomorrow dance.

"Remember our prom, Jerry? Wasn't it perfect?" Selena remembered her mother saying with a wistful sigh. "And doesn't our baby look gorgeous? Who would have guessed she'd grow up to be so stunning?" In the lavender gown, Selena had felt awkward—too tall, too heavy, embarrassed by how the scooped neckline revealed her breasts.

"And you're going to wear this." Annie had slipped her garnet ring onto Selena's finger. "It's a gift. It's yours now."

Selena's heart had swelled. Maybe all her bad luck was about to change. Brent Enderwood was taking her to the Stars of Tomorrow dance! Brent Enderwood!

She'd allowed herself to hope. She'd been sure he'd been seeing Molly Mullin, head of the prom committee, and sure he couldn't really like Selena herself, and yet it seemed to be true. Just as her father was attaching a new flash to his camera—bought just for the occasion—Brent had arrived in his dad's sports car.

What followed wasn't nearly as bad as what happened to Sissy Spacek in *Carrie*, but the second Selena had walked into the dance, hanging on to Brent's arm, he'd led her to the dance floor. Everybody had backed away, laughing. "Did you really think I'd ask a dog like you to the prom?" he'd said.

And then he'd walked away, collecting bets from his buddies. Molly was grinning and waving, turning a full circle for him near the dance floor, showing off a red sheath with a plunging neckline. Now, Selena felt sorry for her. Maybe the only thing worse than being ditched at a prom by a guy like that would be to date him—for real.

Somehow, she'd lifted her chin and headed for the punch table, feeling she had no choice but to brave out the night. Star-shaped candles flickered from tables covered with starpatterned cloths. Despite the splashy decor, Selena had wished the floor would open up and swallow her, and blinking back tears, she'd desperately wanted to call the one man who loved her, her dad. She couldn't share the humiliation, though. Her parents were so proud and excited for her—how could she?

She'd hovered by the punch table, relief coursing through her at the night's end when Chuck Garrison seemingly felt sorry for her and offered her a ride home on his way to an after-prom party. But on the way, he'd pulled onto the shoulder of a deserted back road, and when she'd calmly asked him to keep driving, he'd said he wouldn't until she thanked him properly. He'd kissed her against her will, and when she'd pushed his shoulders, he started fighting back. Even now, she could call up murderous anger at the recollection of his excited breaths, the grotesque groping of his hands over breasts no one had ever touched. She'd punched, hard enough to bruise, and a final swing had raked the garnet ring across his mouth, leaving a deep gash. He'd grabbed the hem of her dress, shoved it up around her waist and torn off her panties.

On top of the sickening fear came the feeling she'd somehow done something bad or wrong, that she was fat and unlikable, that only her parents could love her. Flinging open the car door, she'd tried to run, but he'd pulled her back inside. She'd punched again, kicking his groin, and he'd finally flinched, wiping his mouth with the back of his hand, spitting blood as she jumped out of the car again. "No wonder you didn't have a date, bitch," he'd muttered through the open door. "You're a dog. No one wants you. No one's ever going to want you."

The words didn't sting then. She was too glad he hadn't raped her, too glad he started driving again. Only years later, when she discovered she was too lacking in confidence to make her love life work out, did his words haunt her. Chuck had never looked at her again—not in the school hallways, not when she'd pass him in town—but he'd told people she'd slept with him, that she'd begged him to. That night, she'd walked forty-five minutes toward home, in the dark, on a road with no shoulder, until two women in a truck stopped. They'd been coming from a bingo game, and without her saying much, they'd seemed to understand. After helping her fix her makeup, they'd dropped her under a copse of trees, so her parents wouldn't realize her date hadn't brought her home.

She'd never forget the moments right after that. They were etched in her memory. She could see herself standing in the driveway, recall how the warm, dewy spring breeze touched her cheeks. Taking a deep breath, she'd straightened her face, rehearsed her lies and prepared to tell her folks about what a wonderful time she'd had. It was their night more than hers. They loved the country, and the farmhouse she was looking at was their dream come true. Long after she was gone, they'd be here, enjoying this town....

Maybe when she'd left, she'd been a fool to think her life was turning around. Maybe she'd been a fool to write down her fantasies in *Night Pleasures*, as if that might help her open up, make better choices. Maybe Edison was just a more sophisticated version of the guys she'd grown up with. *Why?* came a voice from deep within her. *Why hasn't somebody loved me yet?*

Blinking, she suddenly realized Dean had continued talking, as Dean always did. "I'm counting on you, Selena."

If Edison *had* betrayed her, she decided she wanted to confront him. Call it therapeutic. People like that didn't deserve her. "Don't worry," she replied, old betrayals mixing with new. "I'll find him."

Calmly—perhaps too calmly—she recradled the phone receiver. Just as calmly, she salted, peppered and ate the three eggs. Determined not to lose her head over a man, no matter how masterfully he'd loved her body, and determined to do things in a rational, step-by-step manner, she began with "I," proceeded to "love," and finally devoured "you."

"GOOD LITTLE BOYS," Selena whispered that night, speaking through the bars of a high, black, wrought-iron fence as she watched the last of Eleanor Luders's four Doberman pinschers roll over and fall asleep in the grass. "Sweet dreams."

As much as she hated drugging the animals, they were lethal, and she'd been assured the pills she'd pressed into the raw ground beef wouldn't hurt them. Besides, she had no choice, since the first thing she'd noticed about Eleanor Luders's estate was that her own black compact car was parked in the driveway. Edison was definitely here.

Selena hadn't arrived until afternoon and, ever since, she'd been watching the house, waiting for dark. "What are they doing in there?" she murmured now, her mind running wild as she checked an equipment belt she'd pulled around her waist, over black leggings and a sweater. Should she have gone inside earlier? Eleanor's security was surprisingly lax, but a break-in during broad daylight would have been a chore. Selena could have disabled the guard at the gate and gone through the front door, of course, but she wanted to enter surreptitiously to see Edison and Eleanor in action. Were the two friends? Enemies? Lovers?

Selena tried to convince herself she was motivated by patriotic duty, not blood lust, but whatever Edison was doing inside, he definitively wasn't making an arrest. She hadn't seen so much as a shadow move in front of a window, and as far as she knew, no one was here but Eleanor and Edison. Of course, Eleanor's husband, a Pentagon bureaucrat, might be here....

"Edison," she muttered in disgust. He'd had plenty of time to share any information he had about Eleanor, including that he'd slept with her, but he hadn't.

"So much for sweet nothings." Taking a deep breath, Selena vaulted over the top of the wrought-iron fence and surveyed the terrain. The estate was incredible, a Frank Lloyd Wright look-alike situated on eight acres of heavily wooded land. Stepping gingerly over the sleeping dogs, then sprinting through the trees, she took in four rectangular, two-story wings, which led to a central sandstone hexagon. Within moments, she'd let herself in through a window.

The interior was breathtaking. Silently, she edged along a hallway, passing modern, irregularly shaped rooms, each more spectacular than the last. Her heart suddenly ached. Dammit, the place was too incredible...a fantasy world. With its mirrors and hallways, it brought to mind her vision of the marquis's palace. Forcing herself to keep moving, she reached an entrance hall with a hexagonal skylight. Through a series of doors inset with stained glass, she could see an octagonal swimming pool, and, tilting her head, she heard voices. *Male and female. Edison and Eleanor.*

"Here goes," Selena whispered. Careful to ensure that her feet were soundless on the terrazzo floor, she crept slowly forward, swallowing hard, determined to confront whatever she found next.

11

WHILE ELEANOR PACED in predatory circles around the straight-back chair to which he was tied, Edison's gaze never wavered. He didn't need to look around. He'd had all day to scrutinize Eleanor's trapezoidal library and consider escape routes, noting exits and gauging the position of the phone on the antique desk in case he could get near enough to call for help. Too bad M wasn't here, he thought dryly. Maybe the dog could have knocked the receiver to the floor and used a paw to dial an operator.

At least the Dobermans had quit barking. Edison figured Eleanor's partner was either feeding them dinner or crating them into canine flight carriers. If Edison could untie himself, he might be able to get through the glass sliding doors and drop over the balcony to the ground without being eaten alive—or without getting shot. About an hour ago, he'd watched Eleanor drop a pear-handled pistol into one of the desk drawers. Weapon-wise, his only hope was a bronze-winged angel perched on a Grecian pedestal. The sculpture was between the sliding doors and the desk, and it looked heavy, easy to grab.

But how could he get out of the chair? And how had

he wound up in this position twice in two days? *Unbelievable.* He continued eyeing Eleanor. She was impeccably dressed in a white pantsuit with a wraparound jacket, her hip huggers fashionably dragging the floor. A rolling Pullman and a steamer trunk were parked by the desk. He tried to make her start talking, hoping to get information that would help lock her away—if he lived. "Leaving town, Eleanor?"

"Maybe."

"Anytime soon?"

"Why do you ask?"

Edison used the only weapon he had—his eyes. They lanced through her. "Because if you are, I wish you'd hurry."

"Cute," she murmured. "You've always had a way with words. I assume you've been using those exquisite verbal skills on your latest conquest. You particularly excelled at sweet nothings, in my view."

Selena was no "conquest," and it grated him to hear what he'd shared with her reduced to the same level as his one rash night with Eleanor. He was in love with Selena. Not that he'd confess that to Eleanor. If she thought Selena was important, she'd use the information against him. Already she'd been trying to wear him down for hours, hoping to find out Selena's whereabouts. "Why don't you just untie me, Eleanor?"

She stopped in front of him, and he couldn't help but flinch as she ran a bloodred fingernail down his cheek. It dropped to his T-shirt, one of Selena's father's, the front of which depicted a peace sign and the words *Cel-*

ebrate Diversity. "Now, now, Edison," Eleanor was chiding, "I'm not leaving until you divulge the whereabouts of your girlfriend."

"Then I guess you're sticking around a while. But then, you might want to rethink that, Eleanor, seeing as the CIIC is onto you. After all, they sent Selena to IBI. She works for them."

"You don't think I know that?"

He shrugged. "Then shouldn't you forget about me and get out of town? I realize I seem like a loose end, but killing me will only make CIIC more determined to find you."

Annoyed by his nonchalant tone, Eleanor tossed her head, her white-blond mane cascading over a shoulder as she widened her stance, planted her legs on either side of his and straddled him. Once seated squarely in his lap, she smiled again. Even though they were eye to eye, she was enjoying the power position. "Tell me where the girl is."

"Why? So you can try to kill her again?"

Eleanor whistled. "Protective, aren't we?"

"Selena doesn't mean a damn thing to me," he lied, careful not to let emotion filter through his words. "But I'd hate to see her wind up dead like..." He wracked his brain for the name. "Bruce Levinson. Wasn't he the other agent CIIC sent? Did you kill him, too?"

Her eyes glimmered with what could only be madness, making Edison wonder how on earth he'd ever mistaken it for patriotic fervor. "Yes," she admitted slowly, "Bruce was getting too close to me." Her already sexy, throaty voice lowered. "And if you don't start coughing up some information, you're going to be next, Edison."

What Selena had told him of her experience with Chuck Garrison flitted through his mind. How did women stomach male aggression? Having such a disgusting woman seated in his lap when his hands were tied gave him a small taste of what harassed women must feel. His voice was calm but murderous. "Get off me."

She merely smiled. "Doesn't this remind you of old times?"

"Old times with you?" He stared straight through her. "That's something I'd rather forget." Right now, his only thoughts were of keeping Selena safe.

Eleanor pouted. "But I made you so hot...."

His blood was definitely flowing faster, but it was pumping with adrenaline that felt like ice. "I don't want any piece of you, Eleanor."

Her tone turned demanding. "Where's your little love?"

It would be a cold day in hell before he divulged Selena's whereabouts to this witch. Wrenching, Edison yanked his wrists upward in an effort to free himself.

Eleanor chuckled derisively, amused by the attempt, goading him. "Keep bucking, and I might get the wrong idea, cowboy," she warned in a fair imitation of Mae West, sending a quick glance over her shoulder as if worried that her partner—presumably her lover—would catch her in the act.

As she drew that horrible red fingernail down Edison's cheek once more, he said, "What about you, Eleanor? Where's your husband?"

"Occupied."

"Are you leaving town with him or someone else?"

"See? I knew you cared."

"I don't."

"Hmm." Her eyes flicked over him. "I'm starting to get some new ideas about how better to torture you. I've always loved tying men up."

"I got that impression from the classified ads you wrote."

She looked pleased. "I, too, have a way with words. Just like you and your friend, Selena."

So she'd definitely written the ads. "Isn't this the second time you've tied me up this week?"

Eleanor merely shrugged. "How *did* you and your whore escape without getting blown to bits?"

He forced himself not to rise to the bait, but he hated the word she'd used, hated that she'd read Selena's passionate diary. "So it *was* you who bombed the house," he replied, wishing he'd never been so suckered in by the lip service Eleanor paid to patriotism and political ideals. Until he'd arrived at her house today, he'd never really believed she'd been stealing from IBI. Deep down, he'd been sure that questioning Eleanor would produce proof of her innocence, and that he and Selena would then proceed to catch whoever was at fault.

Selena. Images from last night clouded his vision. She was in his arms again, her eyes glazed with lust, watching him more openly than any lover ever had. She was parting her lips for another erotic kiss, and he was gliding his hands between quivering satin thighs while she strained her hips, urging him to push his love-slick fingers deeper inside her. His heart clutched. At least he hadn't shared his growing suspicions about Eleanor. If he had, Selena might have come with him today. She could be dead.

Dead.

He couldn't even think it. He'd had a rough enough life, hadn't he? Surely the Fates wouldn't allow something to happen to Selena. Not now, not when he'd found a woman he couldn't live without.

Eleanor was watching him.

"Who was with you?" he prodded, desperate to get a confession out of her, especially since she'd all but admitted she'd killed Bruce Levinson. "Was it the same guy who grabbed me from behind when I got here?"

"Checking out your competition?" she said archly. "Jealous, Edison?"

"Of your lover? Hardly. I feel sorry for him. For your husband, too. How could you do this to people?"

Her red-lipsticked mouth widened, the smile making the cerulean blue of her eyes look less like tropical lagoons and more like polar ice caps. How had he ever thought her beautiful? She was too unreal, too blond, too cold. "No," she murmured, "you never did care about me, did you? You showed no interest in me after I had you transferred to my department."

"You had me transferred?"

"Of course. And now you're too busy with your little girlfriend from CIIC to notice me at all."

"So, you knew she was an operative?"

"Not all along," Eleanor snapped.

"And that's why you bombed my place?" he suggested. "You thought we were teaming up and would catch you stealing from IBI?"

"That's you, Edison. Always the genius."

"You're not going to get away with this."

"Oh, but I am," Eleanor replied confidently. "Our plane leaves shortly. And then we'll catch another plane...and another plane..."

"And get lost forever? Don't count on it."

"There's no proof I've done anything wrong. And I did buy some of those airline tickets on your credit card, which means CIIC might be looking for you. But you'll be dead." She sighed. "Wonder what your little girlfriend thought when she woke up alone this morning?" Her smile vanished. "Where were you two? A motel?"

In heaven, he thought, images of the farm and trailer mixing with those of a star-filled sky and Selena's aroused body.

Eleanor continued. "Wherever you were, you no doubt pleasured her, the way you've pleasured so many." She paused. "Including me."

"Leave Selena alone."

"Nope. I'm afraid we intend to kill you. Her, too. Just in case she really has any evidence against us. I don't much like the wrench you two have thrown into my plans."

Staring at her, Edison became conscious once more of her weight in his lap. The scent of her perfume was overpowering, cloying and thick, and he wished his hands were free, so he could push her away.

Tilting her head, she veered back to study him. This time, it was her thumbnail that found his lips. Brushing it back and forth, she murmured, "I guess our plan to distract you backfired."

"Plan?"

A sudden jerk of her chin dropped a lock of white-gold hair over a glacial blue eye. "Tell me," she murmured. "Did you enjoy Selena's erotic fantasies? Did you like how I forced you to read all that steamy material?" His gut clenched as she dropped a hand down his chest, now flicking it over the fly of his jeans. "Did you get hard?" she taunted.

Sickened, he found himself thinking of the rape Selena had nearly endured, and he clenched his teeth. After a moment, the taut flesh of his cheek quivered. "You mistakenly think I care about her, Eleanor," he forced himself to say, not wanting to hear Selena's name come once more from this foul woman's lips, "but I don't. So, invoking her name while you play this grotesque game with me won't have any effect. Here's the deal. You want me to tell you where Selena is, so you can kill her, just in case she's got any information that could be used to lock you away. But whatever she's got, you can rest assured she'd passed it on to her superiors at CIIC. The way I figure it, you're going to kill me, whether I decide to talk or not. So I might as well save her life. It's nothing personal. I just hate to see anybody wind up dead."

The smile had vanished, her eyes were stone cold, and when the pretty mask dropped, pure fury was revealed. Using all ten bloodred nails, she gripped his collar. "Where is she?"

"You keep asking that." Suddenly, Selena's voice came from behind Eleanor. "And for the past few minutes, I've been right here, watching you."

Gasping, Eleanor whirled just in time to see Selena step through the sliding glass doors. As much as he'd wanted to protect her, relief flooded Edison. He couldn't believe she was here. But she was, dressed from head to foot in black, looking like the most gorgeous cat burglar imaginable. Her hair was pulled tightly back, so it wouldn't get in her way. "There's someone else here," he swiftly warned her. "A man. He and Eleanor blew up my place."

Selena's unflinching eyes darted after Eleanor as she leaped from Edison's lap and made a run for the desk. "There's a gun in the desk drawer," he added. But already Selena was taking care of business. She seemed to be acting in slow motion, not real time—unsheathing the knife at her waist, crooking her arm and raising it masterfully to ear level, then throwing it straight at Eleanor. She'd lost the knife at his place; he guessed she kept a spare.

It arched through the air, the razor-sharp blade glinting as it spun across the room. When it hit, Eleanor stopped, crying out. The dragging cuff of her white slacks was pinned to the floor by the blade, but she'd kept moving, crashing forward with her own momentum, her shoulder catching the Grecian column on the way down. Atop the pedestal, the heavy bronze angel teetered as if about to take flight. And then, like an avenging angel, it swooped down, glancing off Eleanor's forehead. Groaning, she tried to rise, then fell to the floor.

"Selena!" Edison's eyes roved over her as another wave of relief flooded through him. "Hurry up and untie me. Whoever she's been working with is here, somewhere."

"Not somewhere. Right here."

Edison's eyes had been flickering between where Eleanor was prone on the floor and where Selena had moved behind the desk. Now they darted toward the door.

"Carson," he murmured.

Carson Cumberland was framed in the doorway, looking as always like Pierce Brosnan's version of James Bond, with his jet hair perfectly trimmed and his tailor-made gray suit probably bought wherever the president was shopping this year. A striped red-white-and-blue tie was knotted at the collar of a pressed white shirt, and a matching triangle of handkerchief peeked from a pocket. Slowly he raised the gun he held.

But Selena was faster. Eleanor's pistol was in her hand and she shot fast, straight from the hip. "CIIC," she announced in tandem with the shot. "Badge number 7348904."

Carson gasped, hitting the floor, sprawling onto his face, the weapon tumbling from his hand. "Been a while since you've done any field work, huh, Cumberland?" Selena remarked as she moved with lightning speed, circling the desk, crossing the room, kicking the gun from his side. Removing handcuffs from the tool belt around her waist, she cuffed him to the leg of a heavy cabinet.

"Are you okay?" Edison asked, studying where the bullet she'd fired had gashed the wood of a doorframe. She hadn't even really aimed at Carson. Amazing. She'd just disarmed two criminals in under sixty seconds, without even breaking a sweat. Not that he'd support her work for CIIC. He didn't care how good an operative she was, he didn't want her getting killed. "Hey, Selena," he said again. "Now that Carson's down, would you mind helping me out? Eleanor's husband must not be involved. I guess she was running away with Carson."

When Selena turned her eyes to his, he almost wished she hadn't. Their usual spark was gone, and in a heartbeat, he understood. His mind raced back over what he'd said to Eleanor about not caring for her. Had Selena heard him? Believed him? Didn't she know he was trying to protect her?

"Don't push your luck," she muttered. "Dean Meade's on his way. He'll untie you. He said he wants to see you in the security department of IBI."

What? Through the melee Edison had stayed calm, but now his heart was racing. For hours, all he'd done was try to save her life. Didn't she trust him any more than this? Or worse, had their affair been part of her strategy to crack the case? Had she been following Dean Meade's orders to seduce him? Maybe Edison had been played for a fool, and she'd hoped to use him to get close to Eleanor. Narrowing his eyes, he sent Selena a long, assessing stare. Dammit, he knew better than to trust people. "The security department?"

She was heading toward Eleanor. As she leaned down to retrieve her knife and check Eleanor's pulse, he could swear she was blinking back tears, but she said, "Yeah. Dean wants to use the interrogation room in the security office to debrief you."

Dislodging her knife, she carefully resheathed it, those heart-stopping amber eyes panning the room as if she was half-sure she'd forgotten something. And then, clearly intending to leave him tied up in a neat package, she headed for the door, saying the last thing he expected. "Nice working with you, Edison."

"AND YOU NEVER SUSPECTED Eleanor Luders of wrongdoing?"

Crossing his arms over his chest, Edison stared at Dean Meade, wondering if anybody had ever told the man that he looked like a bigger, balder, meaner version of Danny DeVito. Blowing out a slow, murderous sigh, Edison shook his head. Even *he* didn't have a good enough handle on the English language to describe how he was feeling right now. "Sick and shaky" was the best he could do. Sort of like a prizefighter had just pummeled him in the gut. Maybe in a month or so, when he started to heal—if he *ever* started to heal—he'd move on up the ladder to "betrayed." Or "depressed."

Meantime, Edison simply didn't want to be here. Or anywhere else. He shot a glance around the sterile interrogation room, fighting the urge to wave when his gaze landed on the two-way mirror. He'd love to know how many CIIC goons were eavesdropping. All but Selena, no doubt. By now, she was long gone. By now, the sterile apartment where he'd read her diary was probably cleaned out. "Look," he finally grunted. "I told you. I didn't suspect Eleanor or Carson of stealing from IBI. As far as I knew, they were just doing their jobs. Can I go now?"

Dean's beady black eyes narrowed as if he still suspected Edison of purchasing the plane ticket bought with his credit card. Edison sighed. To hell with IBI. To hell with the U.S. Government. Sure, they'd fed, clothed and educated him when he was younger, but now he wanted more out of life than Uncle Sam had to offer. After Selena, one-night stands would never work again. Hell, after Selena, nothing but Selena would work.

Dean was staring at him, looking thoughtful. "Sounds like you're real anxious to get out of here, Lone."

"Yeah," Edison said shortly.

"Mind telling me why?"

Edison shrugged. "Long day. I nearly got killed. Takes it out of a man."

"Lone," Dean murmured. "This is a debriefing, and you need to start talking. Don't forget, I can keep you here for the rest of your natural-born life."

"What's left of it," Edison muttered. Then he added, "Okay. Your operative left me at the scene. I was still tied up. What if Eleanor had come to? What if Carson had gotten loose? I could have been killed. I believe negligence like that is grounds for dismissal."

"CIIC is sorry for any danger you were in," apologized Dean, as if he'd just been nominated the agency's press agent. "But Selena knows what she's doing."

"What?" Edison couldn't help but reply acidly. "Breaking hearts? Seducing people for information?" Even as he said it, he couldn't quite believe it was true.

Dean was still watching him carefully. "Meaning?"

"You didn't need to send her in to seduce information out of me, Meade. If you wanted help watching Eleanor and Carson, I would have worked with your agency. But no, you wouldn't trust your own mother."

"Please, Mr. Lone, we didn't ask her to seduce you. Any seducing she did was of her own volition. We—"

"Maybe it makes sense not to trust your own mother," Edison continued, barely attending to Dean's words. *I really wouldn't know. Mine abandoned me,* he thought. Which was why he never let people into his life, much less his heart. Deep attachments had always been for other human beings, not him. When people got too close, he kept waiting for them to leave him. Which they always did. His father hadn't stuck around, either.

"Anyway," Edison added, "that woman's got my dog. I admit it, I didn't care about M at first. I was trying to find a home for him. But I care about him now. I want that dog back."

Dean squinted. "You say Selena took a *dog*?"

"Yeah. M. He's at her trailer in West Virginia."

"Oh, right," muttered Dean. "I forgot you know the location of the trailer."

Deciding that venting some spleen might feel good, Edison nodded. "Sure do. Which puts her in violation of her CIIC contract. It says she can't divulge her identity without written authorization. So, by rights, you should fire her."

"Mind telling me why you want Selena to lose her job?"

"You figure it out. What do you want me to say? That I love her? That, because my emotions are involved, I really don't want to see her get killed by lowlifes like Eleanor Luders and Carson Cumberland? Is that what you're looking for?"

"I don't *want* you to say anything," Dean answered carefully, shifting his massive weight from one foot to the other, as if he were standing on eggshells. "This is a debriefing. We're simply interested in your view of the events."

"My view is that Selena left me. That's how it looks to me. Okay?"

Dean nodded. "Uh...yeah. I think I got the picture."

"I wouldn't stick it in a photo album," muttered Edison.

Dean ignored the sarcasm. "Can you think of anything else?"

"Other than the fact that I want my dog back?"

There was a long pause, then Dean said, "Yeah."

"No." Edison shook his head. "That's all I have to say."

Minutes later, he was thankfully on the pavement. Being outside should have felt good. Across the street, on a full acre of trees and newly cut grass, kids played and flowers bloomed. When he opened his mouth and inhaled a deep breath, the air tasted as fresh as ground mint. Shoving his hands into his pockets, he cut across the park, taking the nearest route to public transportation. What a day. For hours, he'd thought Eleanor was going to kill him, or kill Selena. Then Selena had left him, and now, wearing a Celebrate Diversity T-shirt, he was taking public transportation to a ruined home he'd worked on attaining for years. He'd experienced worse, though. Been a kid who'd sometimes wondered where his next meal was coming from. As a result he'd locked up his heart and erected guards around his emotions.

But then Selena had come along and broken through those barriers. Now he didn't know what to do. He didn't give a damn about his house or his job—he just wanted her back. Just as a softly uttered "Damn" left his lips, he felt something tugging his pant leg. Glancing down, he saw M. Before he even knew what he was doing, he sank to his knees, his large hands circling the dog's middle, lifting him onto his lap.

Yapping and wiggling, M placed his back paws on Edison's thigh, stretching to press a cold black nose to his face. But Edison barely felt it. He'd realized that if the dog was here, so was Selena.

"Good boy," he murmured, setting M on the ground again. "Stay," he murmured. "Sit."

Just as M rolled over and stuck out a paw to shake hands, Selena said, "Hey."

She'd been behind him. Slowly, he turned, rising to face her. "Hey?" he echoed, the simple, impersonal word reminding him of how he'd felt as he'd left the interrogation room—as if he'd been spit back out on the street without Selena, as if this strange episode in his life was just as fictional as her diary, as if the whole affair had taken place in his imagination. Before he thought it through, he'd traversed the space between them, wrapping his hand around her upper arm, hauling her close. "Hey?" he repeated, astonished. "That's all you've got to say to me?"

She met his gaze, the amber eyes that had been so dazed by lust last night now burning with quieter passion. "I was behind the two-way mirror. I heard what you told Dean."

Edging closer, he pressed his thighs to hers, then wished the physical maneuver wasn't reminding him of every rising degree of heat they'd generated so recently. "Why'd you leave me tied up, Selena?" he demanded, ignoring what she'd said, his voice turning husky against his will, her sheer proximity forcing a traitorous male response that she'd soon feel.

Color touched the perfect cream of her cheeks, and because she'd taken down her ponytail since he'd last seen her, the light breeze was making her hair swirl. "You slept with Eleanor. You didn't tell me."

"I didn't want you to know," he admitted, angling his head down as if to better convince her he cared, his lips hovering a dangerous inch above hers. "I was with Eleanor one night. That's all. But she was my boss, a mentor. I felt I owed her the chance to explain herself. I couldn't really believe she was guilty." Pausing, he fought the urge to unleash a string of curses. "And I was stupid enough to actually think that knowing I'd slept with her might hurt you."

Her lips moved an inch closer. "It did hurt me. In fact, I feel hurt right now."

"And so you left?"

Her slanting eyes were hard to read. He saw love, lust and challenge. "Yeah." Her voice faltered. "I heard you say you didn't care about me."

"I was trying to protect you."

"I can take care of myself."

"Maybe. But the way I feel about you, I want to take care of you, Selena."

Somehow, both his hands had found her, gliding her arms, over her shoulders and under her glorious, silken hair to cup her neck. His body shifted, so their hips locked more tightly. In a breathless second, her slacks brushed his. She molded to him, cradling an arousal he couldn't fight. His words weren't even as audible as the breath he suddenly sucked through clenched teeth. "Dammit," he whispered, "you read my file. You've talked to me. Don't you know what your leaving like that did to me?"

Everything in her eyes said she did. "I'm sorry," she murmured. "I know. I said I wouldn't vanish on you. I promised."

Damn her, he thought. And then, feeling utterly powerless, he simply kissed her. Firm and hungry, his mouth clamped down on hers in a kiss that was meant to capture and never let go. It evoked countless other things, too, such as how he'd felt last night, buried deep inside her. When her lips were good and swollen with the kiss, he leaned back a fraction and gazed directly into her eyes. "Did you hear me say I love you?"

She looked shaken to her soul. "Yeah," she whispered. "And I believe it, too." An impish smile overtook her kiss-slick mouth. "One of the guys was testing a new, state-of-the-art voice analyzer, Edison, and according to it, you love me lots."

Feelings were overwhelming him. He was touched. Annoyed. And starting to regain his sense of humor. He was aroused as the devil, too. Eyes that had been roving over her face dropped to the creamy neck on which he so desperately wanted to rain more kisses. "I do love you, Selena. Didn't you figure that out when I left you those eggs in the fridge? Or didn't you find them?"

There was a sweet catch in her voice. "I found them.

But..." She shrugged. "I guess I thought about high school...."

His lips parted slightly. It had never occurred to him that she wouldn't trust his words. "I love you," he said again.

"You wanted to know why I left," she murmured. "But do you want to know why I came back?"

What loose end hadn't she tied up? "Why?"

"Because I love you, too."

So, *he* was the loose end. His heart stopped, then pounded too hard. An unseen fist seemed to grab it and give it a hard squeeze. *I love you.* It was the first time anyone had ever said those simple words to Edison Lone. "Never leave me," he whispered. "You know you can't do that, don't you, Selena? It'll kill me."

Her gaze meshed with his. "I won't."

What could make him believe it? he wondered. "I don't think words are enough to convince me."

Emotion touched her eyes. "What assurance can I offer?" she whispered, her lips touching his. "I'll do anything I can."

"Anything," he echoed softly, his lips tilting in a smile that matched hers. "You mean beyond sharing more night pleasures?"

"Yeah, what else?"

As he leaned closer, angling his hips to increase their satisfaction, and touching his lips to hers with the kind of deepening pressure meant to make their temperatures soar, he wracked his brain and, genius that he was, came up with the only possible solution. "Marry me."

And chuckling softly, she whispered, "I will."

Epilogue

"ARE YOU COLD, *mademoiselle?*"

"No," Selena lied. She shivered as she stared through the words *HAPPY HOLIDAYS*, which were written in canned snow across a brightly lit bookstore window.

"If you're cold, we'd better go home and get back in bed."

"One more minute." Her shoulders shook with another shudder, but she didn't move away, merely stamped her feet on the sidewalk to keep warm. Suddenly tilting her chin to get a better look at Edison, she chuckled. He was gorgeous, dressed in a navy peacoat, with a black scarf wrapped around his neck. M was tucked under his arm, looking like royalty in a red-and-green plaid doggie coat and wearing wreath-shaped barrettes. Selena's smile broadened as Edison edged behind her, gliding an ungloved hand over her belly, warming it on the wool, where it was full with their baby.

"This is the thing about the greatest sex on earth," he murmured. "There's a snowball effect."

Their snowball effect was due in two more months.

She nodded, loving how his dark eyes sparkled and how snowflakes were catching in his hair, and wishing she didn't have other things to do this evening, in addition to making love. They needed to finish packing, since they were heading to her folks' tomorrow for what would be Edison's first family Christmas.

Could life really be so good? The contractors who'd restored Edison's—and now her—house were finally done, and Edison was once again happy at IBI, since he'd been promoted into Eleanor's position. Carson Cumberland, in an effort to save his own skin, had confessed that he and Eleanor were stealing from IBI. It hadn't helped him. He'd been sentenced to a prison term as long as Eleanor's, and her new husband, feeling betrayed, had offered additional information.

Selena, of course, had quit CIIC to write full-time because Kate was impatiently awaiting the sequel to *Night Pleasures,* which Selena was calling *In Broad Daylight.* Now her eyes returned to the window, and her heart missed a beat when she looked again at *Night Pleasures.* The cover was tastefully done—the jacket red, the lettering white—and stacks of copies filled the window, along with a sign that said Give your True Love the Gift of Sensual Pleasure. Just as Kate had predicted, the books were walking off the shelves. A critic had said, "Silence speaks out in a voice that's daring and bold, with a historical flair that will make *Night Pleasures* a gift for every lover this Christmas."

"Look." Edison pointed. "Someone's at the register."

With a rush of pride, Selena turned and wrapped her arm through his as they watched a distinguished-looking diplomatic type purchase a copy. She could barely believe it. Had she really written a book that strangers were buying? "This is really wild, huh?"

Edison looked as happy as she. He pressed his lips to her temple. "Not nearly as wild as what the author does at home at night with her husband."

Selena looked shocked. "Really? You think she acts out all those lurid fantasies?"

Edison edged closer. "I'm sure of it. I've got inside information."

She cozied up, nuzzling her lips against his cheek, her eyes sparkling with excitement. "You say that as if you may have even met the marquis."

"I *am* the marquis," he whispered.

"Glad to hear it," she murmured, tilting her chin upward for a kiss. When her lips found his, their cold skin quickly warmed.

He smiled. "Why are you glad?"

"Because *mademoiselle* is running through the woods...through the snow..."

Edison shook his head playfully. "And that damnable garter has come unhinged again?"

She whimpered softly. "It's chafing, Marquis."

"We'd better remove it."

"I need a man to help me with that."

With a throaty chuckle, he assured her, "I have the strangest suspicion you'll have one before the cock crows, m'lady."

Groaning, Selena drew a sharp, audible breath, looking shocked. "The cock?"

"Ah, *mademoiselle*." He laughed and, with a slow,

sexy smile curving his lips, took her elbow and began guiding her down the street.

She offered a mock shudder. "Where are you taking me, sir?"

"What about to our bed, *mademoiselle?*"

"Ah, my most exquisite marquis—" Selena suddenly laughed, feeling happier than she'd ever imagined possible "—I can't imagine it being any other way."